COCOONS
IN THE MIDST

COCOONS
IN THE MIDST

An Unfolding Journey
A Choice

KEN KIESEL

XULON PRESS ELITE

Xulon Press
2301 Lucien Way #415
Maitland, FL 32751
407.339.4217
www.xulonpress.com

Unless otherwise indicated, Scripture quotations taken from the Holy Bible, New International Version (NIV). Copyright © 1973, 1978, 1984, 2011 by Biblica, Inc.™. Used by permission. All rights reserved.

Edited by Xulon Press

Printed in the United States of America

Paperback ISBN-13: 978-1-6628-0922-4
Ebook ISBN-13: 978-1-6628-0923-1

DEDICATION

In memory of Pastor Jerry Cook

CONTENTS

PROLOGUE

JAMES HAD NEVER HEARD SO MANY PEOPLE TALKING about a play in his nearly seventy years, nor had he ever read such uniformly generous reviews from critics. And yet, as he crossed the street towards the theatre on a beautiful, sunny day in San Diego, he couldn't recall what this play was supposed to be about. The ticket in his hand was for the 3:00 pm matinee performance. He paused for a moment to glance up at the theatre's marquee to see the title of the play: *Cocoons in the Midst: An Unfolding Journey, a Choice*. He ran a hand through his silver hair as he contemplated why that title seemed familiar to him in a comforting sort of way.

Entering the theatre, he was glad he'd come fifteen minutes early and had a reserved seat. The number of people waiting to get in indicated the performance was clearly sold out. It took a full ten minutes of patiently waiting in line before a helpful young woman serving as one of many ushers could take his ticket and show him to his seat. The auditorium was already full, and the ushers were trying to find space in standing room only areas for everyone who wanted to see the show.

The excited buzz of conversation throughout the auditorium kept rising in anticipation, but when the lights blinked twice to indicate the show was about to start, an immediate and profound hush fell over the audience. As the house lights slowly dimmed, he realized he didn't have a program. He glanced around and noticed no one else had one either. *How very odd*, he thought.

Before he could reflect further on what must have been an intentional decision on the part of the production team, the curtain rose and the lights came up on a stage that was bare except for a young boy, named Jimmy, perhaps ten years old at most, who was holding an old canning jar containing a bright green caterpillar. A wave of recognition and memories washed over James unlike anything he had ever before experienced.

WELCOME!

THANK YOU FOR YOUR WILLINGNESS TO TAKE A journey that spans more than six decades, beginning with a ten-year-old boy, Jimmy, and his comfort companion, a butterfly named Henrietta. We will sojourn with them through the dynamics of living, through the lens of a stage play. Even though the story is primarily about the two of them as they relate to each other and circumstances, there is in fact a third person in the story. *That person is you.*

My desire is that as you witness your presence, it will mirror the potential of your purpose.
Enjoy & Buckle Up!
Ken

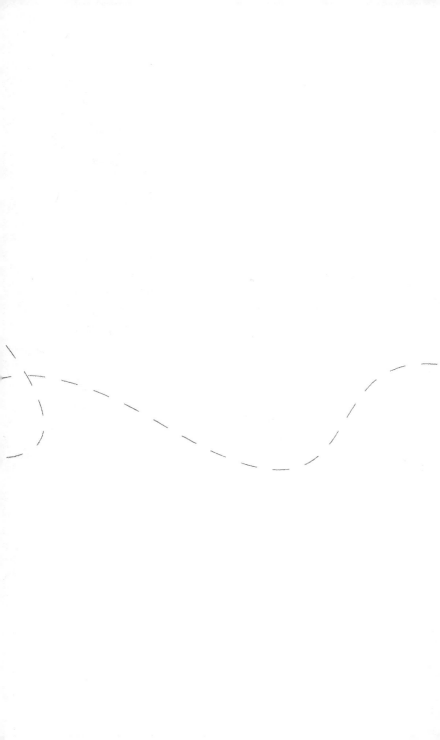

ACT I
JIMMY

Scene 1: FORE!

Jimmy and his family (mother and father, older sister, and two-year-old brother) had just moved into his grandparents' quaint, two-bedroom home a week ago. It had something to do with his dad's job. He and his sister shared a roughly converted garage for their bedroom, with a sheet hung in the center to define their separate spaces. Jimmy didn't mind the accommodations at all. In fact, he was quite happy to be apart from the rest of the family and have such easy access to the property's large back yard, full of all types of citrus trees, and what lay beyond—*his new world*—an abandoned golf course with its meandering stream. High on a hill above the golf course was a church that kept a watchful eye over everything in the valley below it.

On a Saturday free from the drudgery of attending school where he felt lonely and isolated, Jimmy was outside admiring his grandfather's 1953 fire-engine-red Buick parked in the driveway. He was fascinated with what he thought were breathing gills on either side of the front fenders.

Looking across the street, Jimmy saw a rather rotund boy who looked to be about his age playing in the front yard of a house with some kind of metal stick and a small white ball. The boy called him over and Jimmy was curious enough to go meet Dave. The game was golf, and Dave seemed to really love it. He showed Jimmy how his dad had created a putting green in their backyard by sinking soup cans into the ground to create the holes into which Dave seemed to be able hit the small white balls every single time. Jimmy was duly impressed with his skill. But what impressed

Jimmy even more was how much time Dave's dad spent with his son. This was an entirely foreign concept to Jimmy. He couldn't imagine what it would be like to have a dad like that. Decades later Jimmy would see this childhood chum inducted into the PGA Hall of Fame and fondly recall their two years of friendship while Jimmy's family lived with his grandparents.

Scene 2: Over the Fence

At the back of his grandparents' property was a three-foot-high chain link fence, the top of which was eye-level to Jimmy as he was small for his age. To him, making his way over that fence was like walking through the wardrobe in the *Chronicles of Narnia* stories by C.S. Lewis. What lay beyond was seen by others in the community as an eyesore that collected trash blown about by the wind. But to Jimmy the abandoned golf course was his personal five-acre plot of wildlands to explore. Jimmy felt immediately and deeply connected to this place. It may have been unwanted and undesirable to most, but that only made Jimmy love it all the more. And he had it all to himself. It was the only place he could truly call his own, and it was always there whenever he needed it most.

It was this personal adventure land to which he escaped when he wanted to stop thinking about school and how much he disliked it. At school he was called *James*, his full given name. He despised it. His grandmother called him *James* when she was upset with him, which seemed to be all the time as far as he could tell. She excelled at enunciating it with great enthusiasm and volume. What he really wanted to be called was *Butch*, but no one seemed willing to indulge him, least of all at school.

Jimmy was old for a third-grader because he went through second grade twice at his previous school, though he had no idea why. He was fine with it, though, because he liked his teacher, Ms. Manon, who allowed Jimmy to bring all sorts of creatures to school for "share time," which was honestly the only thing that made school even remotely worthwhile. He also felt a certain compassion for Ms. Manon. She had broken her back the previous year and had to wear a cast for a long time. It was never discovered who had pulled her chair out as she was sitting down, but somewhere buried deep inside Jimmy was a voice that accused him of the deed. But he could not hear that voice. Now he was in a different third grade at a different school with a different teacher. He still didn't like school, however.

Scene 3: The Fort

Jimmy quickly found himself setting out on a daily pilgrimage to discover his new world. He was driven by something, though completely unaware of what was driving him or why. All he knew was he *needed* to be out there— exploring, discovering, searching—always searching for something.

At first, his forays into his personal wildland were largely investigatory—exploring the old creek, sensing the texture of the vastness of the wildlife and vegetation. When fully immersed in this place he claimed he found solace and peace. The rest of the world disappeared. Even the noisy traffic on the nearby highway was rendered mute. Everything would hush in orchestrated silence and calm. Then it struck him all at once and he found himself proclaiming aloud:

"I am going to make a fort!"

A wave of excitement washed over him, much like the heightened anticipation when sitting in front of the television waiting with bated breath for his favorite program to begin—*Buck Rogers*. It would be his secret place to collect things from the wilderness and study them.

In this valley tumbleweeds were everywhere. To a boy whose stature was slight, these dried, compressed thistles seemed quite large, and rather intimidating. That night he plotted out his grand undertaking with a to-do list, including all the materials he thought he would need to acquire. As he set about accomplishing this goal, again driven by forces he simply did not understand, it quickly became a major construction endeavor.

Jimmy noticed his grandfather had a collection of poles once used to train up young trees in his citrus grove. No longer needed for that purpose, Jimmy realized the poles of varying lengths could be used to secure tumbleweeds. He assembled the basic shape of his fort with a large central room, much bigger than his "bedroom," with front and rear doors. Using the longest poles to fashion what he would later learn were called trusses, he secured smaller tumbleweeds to form a roof, albeit one that was not waterproof, as he would later discover. All was secured with twine, which he also obtained from his grandfather's bounty.

It was inevitable that the disappearance of so many materials would be noticed. "James," as his grandfather called him, "do you know where all my poles and twine have gone?"

Jimmy chose to say nothing at all, which was his default mode of response. After all, it was vital that the whereabouts of his secret fort remain a secret. In response to his grandfather's inquiry, Jimmy simply shrugged his shoulders, indicating he had no idea what his grandfather was talking about.

Scene 4: Furnishing

With the basic structure of his fort more or less in place, it was time to put his personal imprint on it with furnishings for it to be truly his own. Because Jimmy had no money, his practical strategy was to acquire items that others had discarded, led not so much by knowing what he wanted but by wherever his imagination took him.

The neighboring house to the East of his grandparents' place was enclosed with a fence that seemed to Jimmy to be as tall as the Empire State Building. The man who lived there was always puttering around in his backyard, and Jimmy was very curious as to what he might be doing. He called out "Mister!" repeatedly.

Finally, a fragile, raspy voice acknowledged him, "Yes?"

Words tumbled out of Jimmy's mouth all at once. "I live over here with my grandparents and I'd like to meet you, but my grandmother says you're a jerk and I shouldn't talk to you."

This was apparently enough to make the man curious about this straight-talking boy. "Just go to the gate next to the garage and I'll leave it open for you, but first make sure your grandfather knows where you're at."

Jimmy quickly ran past the kitchen window yelling, "Grandpa! I'll be back in a little while!" and proceeded to go next door. As he passed through the gate, he noticed a whole row of trash cans and a box of jars. "Hello?" Jimmy called out.

The man responded, "Come on in." Making his way to the backyard, he found the man, who was very thin and soft-spoken. Jimmy had the impression he was ill. It was a far different picture than what his grandmother had painted. The neighbor introduced himself saying, "Everyone calls me Bud. What is your name?"

Jimmy quickly responded with a warm smile, as he was now feeling good about his new acquaintance. "James Marvin, Sir. Most people call me Jimmy, but I prefer Butch."

"Butch it is!" Bud said with a smile of acceptance, unveiling his deep furrowed wrinkles. Bud exclaimed with a prideful fervency, "Let me take you on a grand tour into my future!"

Lining the entire backyard on all four sides were tables with boxes on them. Bud went on to explain that he was building a worm farm, as he was going to become a millionaire by selling worms all over the world. The way Bud's face lit up talking about this made Jimmy realize being a millionaire must be a good thing. But the worm farm idea was confusing to Jimmy. After all, he thought worms were only used for fishing, and wasn't sure there were all that many people fishing. Maybe they don't have worms in the rest of the world.

Jimmy told Bud about his project of collecting wildlife from the area but mentioned nothing about the fort. His hiding place must remain top-secret. He also said he should probably return home before his Grandfather began wondering where he went.

As Jimmy started to leave Bud said, "Would you like me to make you a smaller worm bed for your own?"

Without hesitation, Jimmy replied, "Yes! Why Yes! Yes! Thank you!" He thought perhaps he could sell worms all over the world and become a millionaire, too, if his new friend would tell him how.

As Jimmy was leaving, approaching the row of trashcans, Bud awkwardly offered, "If there is anything I can do to help you, let me know!"

Once again, Jimmy didn't hesitate. "What are you going to do with that box of jars?"

"I'm just discarding them." He inserted, "Would you like them? I cannot can with them anymore."

"Yes, yes, yes!" Jimmy said quickly, fearing Bud might change his mind. He didn't understand how jars were once cans. Jimmy picked them up, struggling with the weight of the box, and hid them under his bed. A few weeks later, Jimmy found a miniature worm bed next to Gilbert, his grandpa's red car. A note attached: *Just for you Butch. Your friend, Bud.*

Later yet it dawned on Jimmy he hadn't heard Bud working in his backyard for a long time. His grandfather told him the man next door was gone and wouldn't be there anymore because he had died of lung cancer. Jimmy had no idea why something called cancer would make people move. And the notion of someone having died made no impression on him at all, as if it were an entirely foreign concept to him.

****

Jimmy needed something sturdy on which to arrange the jars so he could categorize the different things he anticipated finding. He noticed an old wooden box in which his grandfather kept his tools. He asked if he could have it. His grandfather said, "No, but we could go to the local grocery store and probably get one, as it used to be a produce crate."

Jimmy seized on this idea immediately. "Can we go, can we go? Please, please, please Grandpa!" He promised he would be good, so good that Grandma would not yell at him. His grandfather chuckled under his breath at the impossibility of that idea. It was very hard for Jimmy to wait until his grandfather was ready to make his weekly trip to the market.

One Thursday morning during breakfast, Jimmy overheard his grandparents talking about going to the market later. Jimmy blurted out, "Can I go, please? Please?" His grandfather's piercing glance told him not to say another word about it or it might not happen. Jimmy was thoroughly distracted throughout the entire school day as he anxiously anticipated going with his grandfather to see about getting some crates.

After what seemed like a century, Jimmy finally found himself on the school bus heading home, though it felt like it was crawling. As the bus came up over the hill and approached the abandoned golf course, the remaining students began their usual routine of telling tales about the place. The stories were ever-changing, at times about there being ancient relics and creatures dwelling amidst the tumbleweeds and other times about the existence of demonic entities that came out at night. This is why the church on the hill overlooking the valley was important. It kept dark forces in check.

Finally, Jimmy's house came into full view and he could see his grandfather standing next to Gilbert. As Jimmy was briskly making his way up the driveway, his grandfather greeted him with his usual salutation, "James, come on! I do not have all day!" Grandpa was always acting as if he had sand in his underwear, always fussing about this or that. Despite this gruff exterior, underneath was a very tall, thoughtful, tender man.

Jimmy was beyond excited. The first phase of furnishing his fort was the box of discarded mason canning jars. This market trip would fulfill the second phase of using crates as chairs to sit on and tables to work on. He was vaguely aware there would be a third phase, though he had no idea what it would involve.

As they entered the market, Jimmy was met with a vast, boldly colored array of items along with an atmosphere infused with smells of food being prepared and lively music. The place was *alive* with sounds and colors and impressions of delight. Jimmy knew that was the impression he wanted for his secret fort. He wanted it to be *alive* in the same way.

As his grandfather went about his task of shopping, Jimmy was fascinated with the selection of produce crates of almost every bright color one could imagine. He spotted a short, round-bellied man working with great intent, wearing what looked like his grandmother's nightcap. Jimmy knew this had to be someone of great importance, probably the owner. He marched right up to the man and asked, "Excuse me, Señor, who paints all the boxes?"

With an inquisitive gaze, the man looked down at Jimmy and broke out into a smile as he explained that the colors were vegetable-based stains applied by his granddaughter, who was about Jimmy's age, in order to help identify the contents of each crate. Yellow for lemons, bananas, and corn, green was for lettuce, cabbage, and celery, and red for apples, strawberries, and rhubarb. Then he asked Jimmy why he was interested.

Jimmy's face took on a helpless expression as he explained how he needed crates to make tables and seats. "Do you have extras I can take?"

With a firm expression the man responded, "No, but I have some discarded broken ones outside by the dumpster and you can help yourself to whatever you can find."

Jimmy immediately sought out his grandfather, who gave him a look that clearly said, "Now what?"

Jimmy tugged at his grandfather's overalls, leading him to the rear of the store, out the back door to the dumpster. The smell out there was intense. Grandpa said, "Let's hurry up. It stinks here. I cannot stand the foul odor." Jimmy, however, did not understand why his grandfather thought it smelled bad. To Jimmy it was an adventure of the senses.

Amidst the spoiled lettuce, rotted bananas, and assorted discarded debris, Jimmy could see different parts and colors of wooden crates. His grandpa said, "I'm going to the car. Come and get me when you're done."

Jimmy began the task of climbing through the mountains of debris to retrieve what he needed. Most people would have experienced genuine disgust, but Jimmy remained focused as he excavated exactly what he wanted. He soon had a pile of pieces that looked like a random rainbow collection of boards. Jimmy retrieved his grandfather and showed him the raunchy assortment, whose understandable reaction was, "There is no way this crap is going in my car."

Jimmy, looking like his favorite kitten had been run over, hung his head and let out a heavy sigh. After a pause, his grandfather said, "Okay, we can go home and get some garbage bags and in the meantime let's borrow Señor Lopez's hose and wash off this mess."

After rinsing everything, they returned home, Jimmy's grandfather lined his entire trunk with plastic and returned to the market with garbage bags. They filled the bags with boards and grandpa reluctantly filled Gilbert's trunk with bags of sopping wet, vegetable dyed wood.

Jimmy knew this collection of boards was very valuable. It also dawned on him that although his grandfather called it "crap," which didn't sound like a word of appreciation, grandpa must have also agreed there was value in the materials. Even old people can change their minds and come around.

Everything was put in the back yard to dry. That night Jimmy could not get to sleep. He was restless and made all sorts of noises. His sister, on the other side of the fabric wall that separated them, proclaimed, "Butch, go to sleep or I will call dad!" That quickly got his attention and he huddled into a ball and finally fell asleep.

Jimmy's presence at school the next day was disruptive as he was focused more on what he would be doing after school. His teacher said if he didn't shape up he would have to stay after school to make up the time he was wasting. The thought of not being able to work on his colored crates right after school absolutely frightened him. To his teacher's amazement, she quickly saw a different side of Jimmy. Instead of what previously seemed like borderline mental retardation, she saw he was capable of being astute, even witty.

She was downright amazed at Jimmy through the remainder of third grade, as well as the following year as she remained his teacher in the fourth grade. In all her thirty years of teaching elementary school, she had never seen such a profound transformation in a student. Twelve years later she was promoted to school district superintendent. After retiring she went on to become a *New York Times* bestselling author on the very same day she qualified for Social Security. She went on to author nine more books, well-known in the field of education and translated in eleven different languages (and four dialects), but the one that started it all was *Discovering Cocoons in Your Midst*.

****

The next few days were some of the most exhilarating Jimmy had ever experienced in his ten years of life. He began putting the assortment of wood in the backyard in order of their color and general condition. He quickly saw he would have to start disassembling some of the crates, sacrificing them to make complete crates.

Grandpa showed up and could see the dilemma—carefully disassembling thin wooden slats while keeping them intact. He disappeared into the garage and came back with a small hammer, a snuffbox of tiny brads (tiny wire nails) and what he called a pry bar with a funny notch in it.

He showed Jimmy how to use the tools. Jimmy learned quickly and set about his task of mixing and matching different colored boards into complete crates. When finished, he had seven beautiful, multi-colored, fully functional pieces of furniture. Grandpa suggested they put a clear seal on the wood to preserve it, as it would be exposed to the elements for the rest of its life. Jimmy wasn't sure what all that meant, but he knew his grandfather was smart so it must be a good thing.

Although Jimmy never revealed what he was up to, his grandfather figured it out easily enough. He'd never seen Jimmy so focused on something, unique for a ten-year-old boy. It reminded him of his own childhood in Germany. Life was unfathomably difficult for his family after World War I, but he was absolutely determined to succeed, to create something out of nothing. He saw this same resolve in Jimmy.

The following Saturday was when Jimmy decided it was time to transport his crates to the fort. There was, however, the matter of getting them over the chain link fence. Once again, without being intrusive, his grandfather suggested that after breakfast he would help Jimmy place them over the three-foot chain-link fence. Without saying a word, Jimmy simply nodded in appreciation.

By nine o'clock that morning all the crates were securely relocated on the golf course side of the fence. Seven round trips from fence to fort was both exhausting and rewarding to deliver each crate to its new home. He was ready for phase three, though he still had no idea what phase three would entail. Sitting in the middle of his fort surrounded by multicolored furniture, Jimmy marveled at what he had accomplished. He had no idea what he was doing. He had simply followed his imagination while making *choices* all along the way.

****

One Sunday afternoon when Jimmy was out and about with his grandfather, they passed a small, obscure business with the word "Pet Land" inscribed on the glass window. "Grandpa, look! What is that place?" His grandfather explained it was the local pet store. Jimmy said with a furrowed brow, "What is a pet store?"

Grandpa replied, "Why that's a place where animals live, it's kind of their home for a while."

Jimmy became very excited. "Can we stop, can we stop?"

"No," his grandfather stated, "it's Sunday and they are not open."

"Oh please, please just stop for a while and look," Jimmy pleaded.

Reluctantly, Grandpa said, "Okay, just for a while. But don't tell your grandmother. She'll have a fit!"

As Gilbert came to a stop in the parking area, Jimmy sensed with mounting expectation he was about to walk through another threshold of some kind. They spent the next few minutes gazing through the glass and Jimmy could not help but think what it was like for all those creatures living in such a tiny place together. It made him quite sad. He needed to go in there as soon as possible.

The next day his grandfather agreed to pick him up from school so they could go directly to the pet store before dinner. The thought of it created great expectations in Jimmy, though he wasn't sure why. When they finally approached the pet store and parked, his grandfather, with a cigarette hanging from the side of his mouth, signaled to Jimmy it was time to get out of the car by raising his eyebrows. Jimmy was very much enjoying getting to know his grandfather better, but he hated the cigarettes. He strongly despised smoking. When his mother would cut his hair, cigarette in hand, he became impossible to work with.

Inside Pet Land, Jimmy just stood there, slowly taking it all in. A very distinguished man with a well-manicured beard approached him, inquiring if there was any way he could help. Jimmy just stood there speechless, finally awkwardly saying, "Hi! Do you work here?"

The man, whose name was Mr. Paladin, said, "Yes, son, this is my business. I am the owner and also the janitor."

Jimmy wasn't sure why being the janitor was important, but it must've been important since he mentioned it. Jimmy knew he needed some kind of containers to hold things he would get from the creek and things he would find in the abandoned golf course. He saw some kind of glass boxes he thought would be perfect. "What are these? Some of them have water in them and some of them have dirt in them, but they look the same." Mr. Paladin explained how the ones with dirt were "terrariums," the ones with water were "aquariums," and how each was used.

When Mr. Paladin told him how much they cost, Jimmy was crestfallen as he had no money or budget. "Do you ever discard them?" he asked expectantly.

Mr. Paladin explained, "There are some that arrive broken. I put them in the back to return them to the manufacturer since I cannot sell them. I'm just waiting for the manufacturer to pick them up but the problem is that I have a new manufacturer and the old one doesn't service me anymore. So I guess I will end up discarding them. Why?"

Jimmy responded, "Well, sir, I need something to put the things in that I find at the golf course and learn how to properly take care of them."

Mr. Paladin inquired, "What kind of things?"

Jimmy suddenly realized this was phase three. This was the culmination of all his hard work so far. He stood still, closed his eyes, and began to recall all the things he had seen over the weeks of exploring his five-acre adventure land. "I need something to put snakes and lizards and spiders and mice into. Would that be a terrarium?"

"Yes, son, and I have some in the back that are damaged. I would be happy to give them to you if it's okay with your parents. But before that, you and I have to have an agreement you will learn how to best take care of what you find and what things are appropriate to confine in your glass boxes."

Jimmy was elated, "Yes, sir! Yes, of course. Will you help me?

They went into the back room and Mr. Paladin found four terrariums of different sizes and gave them to Jimmy. He asked, "Do you have enough room in the house for them?"

"Yes, sir, I have more than enough room. Actually I have a room just for them!"

Grandpa helped him load them into the car and took them home. He even helped Jimmy with the damaged areas by taping over the cracks. He soon had the terrariums placed in his fort. He also became a very regular visitor to Pet Land, where he asked Mr. Paladin an endless stream of questions. Luckily, Mr. Paladin loved to talk about animals. One day Jimmy asked him, "Why do you like animals?"

He began to tell Jimmy the story of how, as a child, he was always fascinated with nature and his dad had a pet store in France where they lived. One day he asked his father why he took care of pets. His dad began to tell him the story of his father's mother:

It was a dark and cold November night in Bordeaux, France, and his family had stoked the stove for the night to stay warm until morning. A spark had somehow found its way to the braided rug in front and began to smolder.

Within minutes, smoke filled the downstairs living area and the family parrot, Caterwaul, lived up to his name and woke the whole family. With minimum damage all was well and his father made a vow to care for the parrot's welfare until he died.

The news quickly spread throughout the village and countryside and within months their house was the residence of other people's parrots. There were soon so many different orphaned companions that he needed to house them away from their home because his wife was very unhappy. He established the first pet store ever in France.

And then Mr. Paladin ended his story by saying, "The parrot over there on the largest perch is ninety-two years old. Can you guess what his name is?"

With a confident smile Jimmy said, "It's got to be Caterwaul! But when did he learn English?"

Mr. Paladin replied, "He never did. Our last name, Paladin, means *guardian*, and we were meant to be a guardian for nature's cause."

Jimmy thought for a moment and said, "I feel I'm supposed to be a guardian over nature, too. Can I do that even though my last name isn't Paladin?"

Mr. Paladin, with a warm smile said, "Why, of course!" He reached over and grabbed a long-handled fish net and instructed Jimmy to kneel before him on one knee. Touching each of his shoulders and his head with the net, Mr. Paladin proclaimed, "I dub you *Sir Guardian of the Abandoned Golf Course!*"

Jimmy could barely sleep that night. He was an official Guardian now of the abandoned golf course! He could hardly wait for school to be out for the summer in three weeks. He worked even harder at school so he wouldn't have to go to summer school. His teacher, whom he liked almost as much as he had liked Ms. Manon in his other school, continued to be impressed with his efforts. There was also a time when Jimmy's grandfather accompanied him into Pet Land that Mr. Paladin remarked how his grandson seemed truly driven by some force to care for creatures. Indeed, his grandfather had to agree as he witnessed Jimmy becoming increasingly distant from people in favor of nature and its creatures.

Scene 5: The Quest

With the end of his third grade year, Jimmy was free to spend his summer days gathering a wide variety of items from his personal wilderness. The most astonishing discovery was on an early Tuesday morning when he heard a continual high-pitched noise that sounded quite distressful. As he approached a dying elm tree, he could hear the cries for assistance more readily, with varied degrees of desperation. Pinpointing the sound, he immediately opened the emergency satchel that he always carried with him. The shoulder bag was a continual reminder of the day he assembled it from things he knew his grandmother would never miss until, of course, she did. Wondering aloud where her bag might be, Jimmy simply shrugged his shoulders. The missing bandages and first aid supplies went unnoticed.

Jimmy gently wrapped an ever-so-tiny, seemingly naked little bird in clean cloth from his grandfather's supply of polishing rags used to keep up Gilbert's flawless appearance. Cupping both hands together, he began the journey, one of what would become innumerable such journeys, to his co-guardian in the cause, Mr. Paladin. And Mr. Paladin himself came to love the sense of expectancy he felt each day as he turned the worn key to unlock the front door of his pet store, knowing Jimmy would come with new questions and new adventures to share with him.

There were the three baby possums who needed immediate care after being orphaned by a coyote who killed their mother. There was an injured snake. There were baby field mice with no mother. There was a lizard who had lost its tail. The list went on and on. Jimmy took his role as Sir Guardian of the Abandoned Golf Course very seriously, as did Mr. Paladin. In fact, the young boy swore to uphold the natural rights of its inhabitants with every drop of blood he had.

As the summer ended, there was a vast assembly of life in his large tumbleweed home, which was filled with the sounds of expressed gratitude. The *Spring Valley Daily Gazette News*, a very small local publication, began running articles about what they dubbed Jimmy's "Rescuing Care Center."

It all started when a customer of Mr. Paladin's was intrigued about the story of a little boy whose mission was to help needy wildlife; he also happened to be the editor of the *Gazette*. This was reported without revealing anything about Jimmy or the whereabouts of his secret place. In fact, this added a sense of mystique to the weekly column that drove a 200% increase in the publication's circulation up to 642 subscribers. The stories were very captivating and true—well, for the most part, as Jimmy did have a very vivid imagination.

His family, oddly enough, seemed not to worry about Jimmy's whereabouts. They trusted he was out of harm's way and were happy he wasn't bothering them. This period of time spent living with his grandparents seemed to be very stressful to his parents.

His grandfather made Jimmy a two-sided ladder by which he could scale their three-foot chain link fence with safety and ease. Every morning he would greatly admire this small boy as he would disappear into the thicket, always turning back to wave his farewell. Grandpa couldn't fathom why the boy was so focused by his cause.

Scene 6: The Capture

On any given day, Jimmy would inevitably find himself excavating dirt, leaves, old logs, and branches in order to discover what lived beneath them. He always carried a few of Bud's discarded mason jars with him. His grandfather had given him an old ball-peen hammer and nails and he used them to puncture the lids with breathing holes.

He quickly realized he needed a well-defined policy by which to operate, not only to preserve what was currently living in his secret fort but also to provide aid and rescue to any creature in harm's way. He decided to capture, after much investigation, what would be safe. After coming into contact with some deadly scorpions, he learned there are only three varieties out of hundreds in the world that are dangerous, and they were living right here. Safety went both ways, for himself as well as what he found.

The summer was coming to a close and Jimmy had a limited amount of time to get everything in place. His collection quickly expanded to include everything from tadpoles found in the still pools of the stream to a trap door spider complete with its fourteen-inch round dirt home.

Capturing the tadpoles required a thoughtful effort. He needed something to catch them in. He remembered what Mr. Paladin used when he performed the dubbing ritual for him to become Sir Guardian of the Abandoned Golf Course—a fish net. Jimmy figured he could make his own. Rummaging through his grandmother's bathroom wastebasket, he discovered a discarded nylon stocking. Using an old metal hanger, some friction tape, and an old stick, he fashioned his own fish net. To be honest, the design surpassed anything he had ever seen.

The tadpoles were very interesting as most had big fat heads with a protruding pointed tail, but some had two tiny feet where the head met the tail. In time, they grew two more feet, lost their tails, and became frogs! This was astonishing to Jimmy and began a whole new series of conversations (well, questions) with Mr. Paladin. "How did that little fish know it was going to be a frog, and how can they live above the water now, and how did they make those decisions and when to make them?" and so on.

Then there were the snakes that lose their skin, a process called "molting." And scorpions who, if you back them into a corner, will kill themselves by lowering their stinger and inserting it into their own body. And bees that defend themselves by releasing their abdominal stinger towards what is presenting a threat, resulting in them dying afterwards.

Jimmy had so many questions and could not understand why these things happened. None of it seemed *logical* at all. Mr. Paladin did his best to reason with the very inquisitive ten-year-old, but sometimes simply said, "We will talk about this later, when you're older," and left it at that.

In response, Jimmy would ask, "When I am eleven?" That would be in two months, and he felt sure he'd be ready for those more difficult conversations, being older.

His undertaking was a much bigger project than he anticipated, especially being in charge as official CEO (Caring Enough Only) of his own *Rescuing Center*, as the *Gazette* called it. But it gave him an amazing sense he was doing something very important that was much bigger than himself. Jimmy was reaching beyond himself and embedding his desires into the needs of others. There was something deeply satisfying about helping injured creatures heal from their traumas.

Scene 7: Henrietta

One Saturday afternoon Jimmy was wandering among the overgrown trees that lined the creek. There was a light breeze, and the reeds were swaying in the shallow waters. This is where Jimmy would collect tadpoles along the bank. He sat down to just listen to the stillness, and closing his eyes he took a deep breath.

When he opened his eyes, he happened to be looking up and noticed a branch that had an odd little sack hanging from it, dangling in the air. He shimmied up the tree far enough to reach the branch and carefully broke the twig to which the little sack was attached. After getting safely to the ground, he went to his backpack and retrieved one of his trusty mason jars to put it in. He knew Mr. Paladin would know exactly what it was. His curiosity got the best of him, so he headed out to Pet Land.

Mr. Paladin told him it was either a "cocoon" or a "chrysalis," neither of which made any sense to him at all. His co-guardian explained how a caterpillar would weave a web around itself and attach itself to something while it waited to emerge as either a butterfly in the case of a chrysalis or a moth in the case of a cocoon. Eventually Jimmy began to understand how the strange little sack was a very special entrapment that allowed the caterpillar to go through metamorphosis, sort of like his tadpoles becoming frogs.

Jimmy was fascinated by this idea of the cocoon, and he always kept an eye out for more of them, other times he would just sit and stare waiting for something to emerge from it. Occasionally the sack would wiggle and move and twist. He wondered what it would be like to be encased that way.

Finally one day there was more movement than usual and suddenly, almost like peeling a banana, the sack opened up and out came the largest, most beautiful iridescent blue butterfly he'd ever seen. Its body was black and from its head extended two long, slender black antennae. Its shiny bright blue wings had black around the edges with small blue dots. Jimmy noticed there was a large notch in one of its wings, which must have somehow been damaged as it emerged from its cocoon. He wasn't sure this newly transformed creature would be able to fly.

He took his new friend to Mr. Paladin, who explained the cocoon had a hole in it so the caterpillar inside could breathe, and then after metamorphosing into a butterfly, it could use a kind of hook on one of its legs to tear that hole wide enough to free itself. He knew what kind of butterfly it was immediately—a blue morpho. But he was astounded Jimmy had found it because it's native to the tropical forests of Central and South America! What was this one doing in California? Jimmy named his new friend Henrietta. This began a new policy: Jimmy would give names to all his newly found inhabitants.

Scene 8: The Birthday Query

Saturday October 22, Jimmy's birthday, arrived in due time. It was a birthday he would never forget as Mr. Paladin had been invited to his birthday celebration that evening. Now that he was eleven and older, Jimmy was ready to start tackling those harder topics Mr. Paladin previously avoided—things about what instinct in nature meant.

After closing Pet Land, Mr. Paladin went home to take care of the members of his family—a fish named Grubber, a cat named Misty, a dog named Grunt, and a guinea pig infamously known as Miss Piggy. These household companions were his family since his wife's death three years ago.

Having properly attended to all, he went about affixing a blue and white polka dotted tie to a clean shirt, went into his den to retrieve a colorfully wrapped box about the size of a mailbox, grabbed his keys and headed out the front door. When he arrived, Mr. Paladin was duly impressed with the shiny red car in the driveway. He would never have guessed it was so old. It looked brand new to him.

Jimmy ran out to greet Mr. Paladin and noticed him admiring the car. "That's Gilbert, my grandpa's car." Mr. Paladin wondered aloud about the name of the car, "Gilbert because it looks like breathing gills on both sides of the fenders?"

Jimmy exclaimed "Yes, exactly! How did you know?"

Mr. Paladin said it made sense to him. Jimmy's grandfather met them at the door and began to introduce him to Jimmy's mother Alberta, and grandmother, Gertrude. Jimmy's sister was at a friend's house, his younger three-year-old brother was down for a nap, and his dad was at a very important meeting at John's Tavern.

It wasn't much of a birthday celebration—just a few cup cakes with Jimmy's having a candle. Jimmy didn't think much about it because it was the same as all his other birthdays. Mr. Paladin, however, coming from a French upbringing, expected something much more elaborate. But it didn't matter as his focus was solely on Jimmy.

Jimmy received a grand total of four gifts. His mother gave him a set of six new socks, all black. His grandmother gave him a book on proper etiquette for children when they're with adults. Grandpa's gift was the smallest of them all, and yet surprisingly heavy. Removing the wrapping paper revealed a wooden box (later revealed to be walnut). Inside was a shiny brass circle with a clear glass cover, a kind of clock face unlike Jimmy had ever seen, for it had only one hand that seemed to be continuously jiggling and shifting about.

His grandmother blustered out with displeasure at Jimmy's grandfather, "Bill, I can't believe you spent that much money! We can't afford it with so many of us living together trying to make ends meet!"

Taking the outburst in stride, he explained he was giving Jimmy a gift his grandfather gave him when he was eleven—a mariner's compass. It had been a tradition over three generations and when Jimmy eventually had a grandson he would be expected to keep the family tradition alive. "With this compass you will never get lost," he told Jimmy, giving him a big smile and a kiss on the cheek. Jimmy loved that, despite the smell of cigarettes reeking from him.

Every adult in the house was a chain smoker and Jimmy was very thankful he did not have to be around it all the time since his room was in the garage. His sister didn't seem to mind the smell of cigarettes but hated living in the garage. She was ashamed to have any friends over.

The last and final gift was the very large and heavy one from Mr. Paladin. As Jimmy began to unwrap it, he could see a picture on the box of one of those glass boxes. "It's one of those aquariums or is it a terrarium?"

Mr. Paladin said it was either, depending how he chose to use it. He said he had purchased it weeks ago to give to Jimmy so he would have one that was brand new and not damaged, perhaps to be used for a special endeavor.

Inside the glass box was a book on spiders from Time-Life libraries. Jimmy would receive another such book every month for two years, all about different aspects of nature. The pictures were amazing, though the words were very difficult to make out as reading was hard for Jimmy. It was by far the best birthday of his entire life so far and would be for many years to come. He could barely go to sleep that night from the joy he felt.

Scene 9: The Disclosure

The Wednesday after Jimmy's birthday, his grandfather informed him he would be picking him up from school instead of getting on the bus. Earlier in the week, he had gone by the local produce market and talked with Mr. Lopez, the owner, and arranged for Jimmy to come and get a brand-new crate of his own. His grandfather thought Jimmy should have a stand that was worthy of holding Mr. Paladin's gift.

Jimmy's mind was a jumble of possible explanations as to why he might be in trouble, which was the only reason he could think for his grandfather picking him up from school, which almost never happened. *There was that incident last week with this mouthy girl named Alice, who was responsible for the school bus driver pulling over and stopping. It would have been different if what she said was true. What she announced to everyone in a very obnoxious manner was how my golf course was stupid and so was I.* Jimmy couldn't have foreseen how Alice would join he and Dave in a trio like the Three Musketeers, becoming inseparable over the next few years, even though they all moved several times.

Although a surprise was awaiting Jimmy, it was not a bad one. His grandfather took him to the market to pick up a brand-new, never-before-used produce crate for his brand-new terrarium. Mr. Lopez's granddaughter, Cecelia, had just finished dying it a vibrant blue, especially for him. Jimmy knew immediately that this was Henrietta's new home. He couldn't wait to put the brand new blue crate with the unblemished terrarium as a private *casa* for Henrietta's dwelling.

Jimmy was beginning to feel the weight of keeping his fort a secret and felt a growing desire to share it with someone. He considered Alice, who had become a steadfast friend. But no, there was no one more deserving of sharing his secret than Mr. Paladin. When he explained everything to Mr. Paladin during his next visit to Pet Land, he was surprised at his response. Mr. Paladin was absolutely honored to serve as a partner in the project in a back-up sort of way. He asked Jimmy to put directions and specifics in a sealed envelope for him to access if ever he needed to. In other words, Jimmy was able to share his secret while still keeping it a secret. Brilliant! And he used his trusty mariner compass to create very specific directions for finding the fort.

****

Jimmy was deep into the next phase of his project, which was dividing the remainder of the unexplored wasteland into grids, with longitude and latitude reference points in order to find and record by journal what was gathered. On the Saturday before Thanksgiving, Jimmy was planning to document the last unexplored quadrant of the golf course. He took nothing with him other than his journal, pencil and compass. He started out early in the morning to take advantage of as much daylight as possible. Filled with anticipation, he forgot to take any food, only water. The area left to plot was desolate and dry, filled with a lot of small twiggy underbrush and a withering oak tree. Jimmy went all day

32

and half the afternoon, but for the first time in over thirty-nine expeditions, he came up empty-handed in terms of collecting anything new.

He was about to call it a day when his eye casually encountered a tiny ball of what looked almost like fur with a rich brown and amber appearance. Scooping it up in his hand, the ball unrolled and started crawling up his arm. Caterpillars! Maybe they liked the leaves of the oak tree. He gathered up several of the creatures, along with some of the oak leaves and took them to his fort and secured them in one of his mason jars. He had to hurry home as it was getting late.

The next morning Jimmy returned to the final quadrant to explore it more thoroughly. Right away he noticed a bright green plant that stood about two feet tall with flowering leaves all over that he was quite sure hadn't been there yesterday. Upon scrutiny, he saw a large green caterpillar that didn't have any fur on it. It was smooth, shiny green with small white spots. He took it and the plant back to his fort to add it to his collection.

These caterpillars were his last acquisition, so he used one of his terrariums to be their home. He named all sixty-three creatures living in his fort. But Henrietta was always his favorite. Each time he arrived to the secret fort he greeted her. And his final act before leaving the fort each time was saying goodbye to her. How he knew or decided Henrietta was a "she" remains a mystery to this day.

Scene 10: The Pain of Death

One gloomy morning, a rare occurrence in San Diego, Jimmy spotted his grandmother's cat, Margaret, thrashing about at the base of an Oleander bush. After hearing an unforgettable screech ebbing into silence, Margaret swaggered forth from within the bush, holding tightly in her jaws a large limp mouse. She quickly scampered away to consume her catch.

Jimmy had just witnessed, for the first time in his life, *death* and it was nothing short of distressing. The next few moments transposed into a long, quiet pause and a deep aching in his stomach that suddenly forced him to make a quick visit the bathroom.

After splashing his face with water, Jimmy returned to the bush to offer his final condolences to what he had encountered. As he turned away to get ready for the school bus, he heard a faint squeaking, one like he had never heard before. Kneeling before the Oleander bush, he began to see pieces of cotton and string, a bird's feather, and a collection of straw, all in a pile, along with a faint movement from within it. Reaching in ever so carefully he unfolded what looked like a very deliberate structure, revealing three naked field mice that were probably only hours old.

He quickly ran into the house to his grandmother's bedroom as she was in the bathroom flossing her teeth (and Lord knows it took her forever to floss her teeth). He went into her closet and found an empty shoebox. Going into the garage, he remembered where grandpa had put gardening tools and grabbed a small gardening trowel. He lined the shoebox with clean rags and, wielding the gardening trowel like a sword, Jimmy gently scooped up the orphaned castaways.

It was getting late and Jimmy needed to find a warm, quiet, dark place to provide comfort to his new charges. He decided to return his grandmother's shoe box to where he originally found it (his grandmother was *still* flossing her teeth). Placing the lid on top, with breathing holes he had punched into it, he also took the top off a catsup bottle, cleaned it thoroughly, and put clean water in it so they would have something to drink.

He grabbed his backpack and quickly ran up the hill as the school bus was approaching his designated stop. He was thoroughly distracted all day long at school, resulting in his teacher sending him twice to the nurse's office as he seemed to be in some kind of trance. Of course, he must just be thinking about his new charges.

When the school bus finally delivered him back home, he sprinted to the house. Entering through the side door into his garage-bedroom, he could hear his grandmother screaming at his grandpa. "William, William, come here immediately!" Unbeknownst to Jimmy, she kept all her shoes in individual boxes, although some of them were empty. By some twist of fate, she had picked up the very box containing the newly birthed and freshly orphaned baby field mice.

"That G*&D@#* kid! What has he done this time? Go get a bucket and flush these dreadful things down the toilet!" In an instant, Jimmy could hear a rumbling in the garage and the horrible sound of a flushing toilet. His heart simply sank. He walked to the far end of the backyard, next to Bud's fence, peeping through a knothole while tears ran down his cheeks.

Scene 11: Disappointments

This started a new season, one in which he would not speak to or even look at his grandfather, the murderer of the helpless field mice and in whom Jimmy was thoroughly disappointed. Although he took no other actions against the executioner, he did seek revenge against his grandmother. He slowly began replacing small amounts of the sugar she put in her coffee with salt until eventually the sugar bowl contained ninety-percent salt. To his utter amazement, she exclaimed this new brand of coffee was the best she ever had and instructed Grandpa to buy a whole case.

As time passed, Jimmy found he was losing interest in his secret place, and his visits to Mr. Paladin became increasingly sporadic. On one such visit to Pet Land after an especially long absence, Mr. Paladin exclaimed, "Sir James, I have missed you! Come here and let Uncle Pal give you a big hug!" Jimmy practically collapsed into Mr. Paladin's arms and began to sob, quietly at first, then with greater force, as if a dam had finally given way. Mr. Paladin held him until the heaving sobs receded, saying nothing. Jimmy felt so much better afterwards. He felt truly comforted by the hug. This was a whole new experience to him—feeling close to and comforted by another person. The whole exchange was very foreign to him, and yet he was grateful for it, as it served as an emblem for what he cherished as valuable throughout his life.

****

During the months that followed, Jimmy witnessed many events at his fort. A lizard died, a snake ate a spider, and caterpillars wove cocoons for themselves. The frogs disappeared one by one, leaving only the king snake. This was the natural workings of the food chain, but Jimmy still found it all perplexing and distressing. As always, Mr. Paladin was there to intervene gently and informatively with his hearty laugh and calm demeanor. It was only natural Jimmy would come to rely on him more as a source of life guidance than his grandfather, the murderer.

Then one Thursday when Jimmy entered Pet Land, he found Mr. Paladin studying a letter, deep in thought. He seemed distracted and solemn. Jimmy couldn't help but wonder what was happening. Mr. Paladin explained how his son, with whom he had not been in contact for many years, was supposed to come for a visit but had to change his plans. Jimmy didn't know he even had any children at all. As it turned out, he had five children. He was so looking forward to reconnecting with his son and was now very disappointed it wouldn't happen after all.

Scene 12: Steeple on a Hill

Jimmy was often curious about the symbols he saw in Mr. Paladin's store and home. One evening, Mr. Paladin invited Jimmy to share dinner with him and his "family." As lovely as it was to spend time with Grubber, Misty, Grunt, and Miss Piggy, what really fascinated him was an old, dusty statuette on the dining room table.

Cooking was a rare event since his wife died, and all the animals seemed excited it was happening this evening. Before they began to eat, Mr. Paladin bowed his head and with one hand touched his forehead, then his chest, and then each shoulder. Jimmy had never seen anything like this before and upon inquiring found out Mr. Paladin was Catholic, though he didn't know what that meant.

By night's end, however, Jimmy understood it a little better. It seemed to involve going to a place to honor his wife's memory every year on their anniversary. Mr. Paladin used to go every week with her, but since her death only goes once each year.

****

Soon it was the end of August, which also meant the end of another summer and new school year on the horizon. As usual, everyone seemed occupied with their own endeavors, making it quite easy for Jimmy to slip over the fence and into his world. No matter how many times he had made this quest it always retained the thrill of his very first time.

He often consumed his breakfast rather quickly so he could escape into the day's adventures.

Each time he entered his private world, he deliberately paused in order to sense what he would do that day. Jimmy's breathing would slow as his mind would scan the environment to map his direction. Thanks to his trusty mariner compass, he had developed a finely tuned internal GPS such that he eventually had no need to use it at all.

On this day, his gaze settled to the far south end, to the elevated area overlooking the valley. Yes, today he would venture where seemingly "*No man had ever gone before.*"

It was a dry, warm day with a significant breeze pushing its way from the pinnacle above the valley. At the top was the strange building with a structure atop it that pointed to the sky. Deciding to go there would take him where he had never yet ventured in his private world. He felt a mix of both anxiety and anticipation.

The trek was taking much longer than he expected it would. It was already midday and the hot sun was directly overhead. He took a sip of water from his Davy Crocket canteen, wiped his brow with a sandy handkerchief from his back pocket, and determinedly resumed his quest without knowing what was pushing him to reach his intended destination.

At last, he finally reached the far end of the valley and only needed to complete making the ascent to the strange building at the top. When he reached the half-way point of his climb, he sat down and looked back at the valley below. His tumbleweed fort was looking very small from this vantage point. He noticed strange imprints in the rocks around him, like tracks, but they seemed mysteriously different and otherworldly. Had he found evidence of an alien presence? He marked the spot with a pile of rocks and a dead branch sticking up out of it so he could find it again.

Resuming his climb, Jimmy started seeing gray lizards sunning themselves on huge boulders. Scaling these boulders was no easy feat, but Jimmy had to find a way to do it to reach his destination. After several tries, he got the hang of it. He also managed to nab two lizards along the way, which he placed in separate containers he carried in a pouch that he wore around his neck. The two lizards looked identical except one had two yellow stripes on its belly and the other had two blue stripes (he would later learn the yellow-striped lizards were females and the blue-striped lizards were males).

Suddenly a man's voice was shouting at him. "You there, boy, get off the rock!" Jimmy was startled and nearly fell, though he was more concerned about squishing the new-found additions to his family than himself. The man approached Jimmy and extended his hand, saying, "Let me help you." Jimmy accepted his invitation and made his way off the rock. The man was dressed all in black except for a little square of white at his throat. He seemed very official and Jimmy knew he must be in big real trouble.

When the man asked what his name was, he did so with a gentleness that reminded Jimmy of his grandpa—not at all like his dad. Jimmy asked what his name was and he said it was John. Jimmy didn't know how to ask politely about his clothes and blurted out, "Why do you wear black? Are you sad?" Jimmy had a vague memory going to the funeral of someone he didn't know. Everyone wore black and seemed unhappy. There was a lot of crying and hugging. The man said, "No, I am not sad. My attire is worn to honor my boss."

Jimmy's next question was inevitable. "Who is your boss?"

And so began the first of what would become a series of regular conversations with John. Jimmy learned John was the Pastor of this church on the hill. It took Jimmy awhile to understand what being a pastor meant and what he did in order to become a pastor. To Jimmy it seemed like it was about convincing people, like when his dad used to sell appliances, which was what he did before they moved in with Grandpa and Grandma. But he was so different from his dad. John would actually *speak* with him and ask *him* questions. Dad either ignored him, yelled at him for what he did or didn't do, or put him off with, "Not now, boy."

Jimmy entered yet another new era, one in which he looked forward to his weekly conversations with pastor John. Jimmy was always surprised at how John seemed genuinely interested in what Jimmy was doing—about his fort, his crates, his mason jars, and his glass boxes. But the most amazing thing of all was how John seemed to know where all the creatures Jimmy had acquired came from. It was his introduction to the concept of God the Creator.

One afternoon when Jimmy was having one of his talks with his new friend John, he felt a sudden shivery feeling near his neck and the pastor suddenly exclaimed "Look at that! There's a huge blue butterfly on your shoulder!" It had been weeks since Jimmy had tearfully set Henrietta free, along with the other butterflies who lived in his fort. He knew he couldn't feed them properly and didn't want them to die. Feeling a wave of comfort and solace from her presence, Jimmy explained calmly to pastor John, "This is my friend Henrietta. She's very special." Pastor John could only nod his head in wonder. A moment later, Henrietta fluttered off to parts unknown.

In retrospect, these three men—Grandpa, Mr. Paladin, and pastor John—each served a very specific purpose in Jimmy's life. His grandfather was a true patriarch of stability. Mr. Paladin had extensive knowledge about animals. And pastor John, with his quiet demeanor, always left Jimmy feeling calm, cared for, and comforted. Each of them saw how driven Jimmy was in his cause of caring for the hurt and distressed creatures of his private world. None of them however, could ever surmise the root source of Jimmy's drive, which was something that would reveal itself 40 years later.

ACT II
WINDOWS IN TIME

Scene 13: Leaving Home

It was one of those evenings when Jimmy's father saw fit to share his continual displeasure with his older son. "You G*d D*mn kid, you'll never amount to anything!" The conversation increased in volume and intensity to where Jimmy made a decision. He was seventeen years old and he was *done*. He didn't know exactly what this meant or what he was going to do. He just knew this scenario was extremely abusive, probably for both of them.

Yelling even louder than his dad he said, "That's it!" He swung open the patio door, crossed the backyard, and hopped over the fence. The house was set on the edge of a canyon, and even though Jimmy was barefooted, he ran— with no intention of coming back.

All he could think of was a lady he'd met who took kids into her home. Jimmy had been attending a local church lately where she was a member and they had spoken a couple of times. He was fascinated with her compassion. To be honest, the only reason Jimmy went to church was to meet up with his girlfriend. He worked after school during the week and all day on Saturday, which made Sunday his only free day, and Sundays meant his girlfriend would be in church, so if he wanted to see her, he needed to go to church.

After running a couple of miles, Jimmy approached the front door of Marjorie's house, the lady who took in kids who needed help. She could see he was distressed and asked him to come in. She saw his feet were bleeding and told him she would first take care of that. Afterwards, because it was late, she gave him a pillow and some blankets and let him sleep on the living room couch for the night. The next morning, they sat down and talked for a long time. She simply asked, "How can I help?" Jimmy explained how he simply couldn't go home, and it was true. He didn't visit his parents until years later when he was married and had a family of his own.

A plan was put in place, but because he was only seventeen and technically a minor, she asked permission to contact his parents. Jimmy declared, "You can talk to my mom, but do not speak with my dad." After finishing a phone call with his mom, it was decided he would stay with Marjorie for a while in order to bring some objectivity to the situation. The next day she drove him home when his parents weren't there so he could gather up some clothes and personal effects.

That afternoon, everyone else had gone to the beach but Jimmy decided to stay back. Going out to the backyard, he just sat on the grass under a large tree, thinking of all that had taken place. A light breeze came up and felt good against his face. There was a bird bath on the edge of the property, near where he was sitting. Perched on the edge of the birdbath was none other than a large, iridescent blue butterfly! Jimmy couldn't help but think of Henrietta. Of course, it couldn't be her. Henrietta had come into his life years ago, back when he was obsessed with his secret fort and adventuring in the abandoned golf course. But there it was in plain view—a blue morpho butterfly. Jimmy couldn't help himself. He approached the birdbath to get a closer view, and then he saw it—the unmistakable notch on the edge of one wing. It *was* Henrietta, improbable as it seemed. Taking flight, she hovered before his eyes for a moment, as if greeting him, before fluttering off. He felt immense peace and comfort in the midst of his turmoil to see his old friend. Seeing Henrietta touched him deeply, giving him hope.

****

A year-and-a-half went by and Jimmy had lived with two other families within the church. The one family had a little five-year-old girl who could not talk or walk. The mother was doing a new kind of therapy called "Patterning" to try and affect the brain's pathways in such a way as to create normalcy in speech and walking.

The second family he stayed with was the family of the church elder, who fortunately was very kind. Jimmy, however, managed to cause a good deal of turmoil in the house. There was an outside bathroom where Jimmy used a product called Butch Wax on his hair. One day it fell out of the cabinet and broke the sink! Then there was the Halloween party. He came up with the idea of having a skeleton drop from the hallway ceiling as kids made their way to the party. It was a great idea, but the execution was lousy. He found out the hard way what happens if you don't carefully keep your feet on the trusses in the attic—you end up crashing through the sheetrock to the hallway below, along with all the blow-in insulation. Wilda, the wife, in a summer dress, was quite immersed in debris and insulation. Needless to say, they were so elated when it was time for him to go to college that they threw him a rather exuberant going away party.

He had been baptized and accepted Christ as his Savior, not that he had any idea what it really meant. He mostly did it to impress his girlfriend. He generally saw the process as a means by which he could be a good person and do things right. And Lord knows by that time, he sure needed that. But as he decided to get more serious about it, the first thing he had to do was break up with his girlfriend, as they had developed an inappropriate sexual relationship that didn't seem to fit his notion of being "good" now that he was a believer.

Things took an interesting turn one night at the Youth Meeting. A young woman named Laura, who worked for an attorney, told him, "Your dad called my boss today." Apparently his father was aware of how Jimmy had committed himself to this thing called "Christianity," and wasn't having any of it. He was seeking legal counsel for suing the pastor who had baptized Jimmy. Jimmy and his dad, to the day he died, never spoke of this strange episode.

Scene 14: College

There was a local Christian college in Los Angeles called Pepperdine, and after talking with several people, Jimmy decided he should attend. He had been going to a local Junior College but lacked direction. He sold his car, got on a Greyhound bus with his ten-speed bike and off to college he went.

After his second year in college, he found out one day while eating lunch with Mr. Moore, the Comptroller of the college and his boss, that his father had filed a lawsuit early on to stop him from attending Pepperdine. When Mr. Moore saw Jimmy had no financial support at all from his family, he decided to approach the Board of the school to see if he could have financial custody to make decisions for Jimmy, as a parent would. He also sought approval from his wife, since she would essentially become a responsible party as well. They were discussing it one day on their patio with all the legal paperwork in front of them, trying to decide what to do. They knew if they didn't, Jimmy would never have a chance at a college education. But it was a big decision.

At that moment, a large, gorgeous, iridescent blue butterfly landed on the edge of the table where they were sitting. It paused for a moment, then took flight. They both thought it was going to fly away, but instead it made a few circles and then came back down to land on the pen lying next to the paperwork. Mr. Moore's wife exclaimed, "It's a sign!" As the butterfly took off again, they both noticed a significant chunk missing from the edge of one wing. They marveled at how the beautiful creature could even fly!

Jimmy was nothing short of astonished by Mr. Moore's story. Of the 2,500 other students attending Pepperdine, how was it that the Comptroller saw fit to take him under his wing. Mr. Moore explained, "If there's anyone who wants to sue to keep his kid from going to my school, I knew I had to meet that kid and help."

At the end of their lunch, Jimmy said, "Well, if you ever happen to see that beautiful blue butterfly again, you can call her Henrietta. That's her name." Needless to say, Mr. Moore wasn't quite sure what to make of that.

Jimmy was unaware that Mr. Moore had co-signed on a student loan to fill in the gaps in Jimmy's tuition. Ten years after graduating and dutifully making his monthly payments, Jimmy received a letter from the Bank of America saying his loan was PAID IN FULL, and saw what was familiar to him, Mr. Moore's signature as the Guarantor.

Scene 15: Unspeakable Loss

During college Jimmy had married a woman named Mary Jane. Because they had their wedding in a church, Jimmy's father refused to attend. After graduating, they were living in Perris Valley, California. Like Marjorie when he was a teenager, he and his wife took in teenagers who needed guidance and positivity in their lives. At the time, there were nine teenagers living under one roof.

On one particularly beautiful autumn day, everyone was gone, leaving him to his own devices. He took advantage of the situation to spend time in the neglected olive grove on their property. Going there reminded him of the abandoned golf course from his childhood. Something about spending time in these types of landscapes was helpful to him. It somehow pushed him along the path toward wholeness and meaning. The Olive Grove was a special place. Because it had been abandoned for many years, there was a wild look about it. The air was still and there was a unique odor that lingered in the air, something that only emanates from Olives trees. It was the perfect place to sit and contemplate.

Their first child was only weeks away and there was much to consider. One thing Jimmy knew for sure—he was determined to be a father very much the opposite of his own. the one that he had experienced as a child. A breeze began to pick up and find its way through the overgrown branches of the trees that overlooked where he was sitting. He found himself transported back in time to the days of the golf course, the time he spent with Mr. Paladin, and his journeys to the steeple on the hill. Most of all, he thought of Henrietta.

For the first time, he pondered his encounters with her in such a way as to see some patterns. Although she appeared only infrequently, Jimmy realized he had the overwhelming sense she was always there with him, his constant companion. He was never truly alone. The unique sense of peace and comfort that seemed to follow him he attributed largely to Henrietta's presence in his life, whether seen or unseen. She was always watching over him, and he always felt cared for. She was like his personal guardian angel, as if she had his back. He never spoke with anyone these days about Henrietta, not even his wife. He was not sure what others would make of this unique partnership from which he gained so much.

****

Many years somehow flew by in which they had spent time at Children's Farm Home in Galveston, Texas; Teen Challenge of Southern California in Riverside; Tajunga Home for Boys; Saint Mary's Home for Boys in Beaverton, Oregon; Anthony Achievement House in Forest Grove, Oregon; and Specialized Out of Home Care (SOHC, a federal grant project) in Gresham, Oregon. Jimmy and Mary Jane now had three boys, with one more on the way.

It was a gorgeous Fall day with a crisp breeze, bright sun, and large billowing clouds. They entered the office of the doctor who would be delivering the baby in about a month. All these years they had never had health insurance, as they were independent contractors with the different groups that employed them. They were on a payment plan with the doctor, and their regular $47 payment was due that day.

The inside office had the most amazing terrarium that was open to the outside by having a movable roof assembly. The unique thing was that it had a glass door leading into it from within the office. It was about eight feet by eight feet in size, and their boys always looked forward to going along on these appointments as they absolutely loved to go inside it to play.

They really liked the doctor. He had recently completed his hospital internship and now had his own practice. This would be his first baby he'd delivered outside of the hospital internship. It was obvious he was embracing his new adventure with enthusiasm and confidence. After concluding the visit he smiled and said, "Well, see you next week!"

They went to the indoor terrarium to gather up the boys. The middle child, the mischievous one, was trying to catch butterflies. Jimmy and his wife always said if they'd had him first they probably would've never had another child. He was such a delight, but also a handful! Jimmy's mother used to say he was very much like him when he was his age.

They sat down with the boys, endeavoring to curtail the butterfly collecting. The youngest, the quiet one, held up his arm and said, "Look!" He was a child of few words to begin with and hardly spoke at all until he was almost three years old. On the back of his arm was a large iridescent blue butterfly sitting still and calm even amidst the surrounding chaos. Jimmy could see at once it was Henrietta, though he said nothing. What felt like a long time just marveling at her presence, she fluttered up to the top of the terrarium, pausing as if to say goodbye, and then disappeared.

No longer able to contain the wave of emotion welling up inside him, Jimmy burst into tears. They quickly made their way out to the car and left. On the way home, Jimmy was still crying. The boys kept asking, "Is Dad okay?"

At first, Jimmy thought he had been caught up in the moment of seeing Henrietta again. But then for weeks afterwards he found himself very emotionally fragile, crying at the drop of a hat. His sleeping hours were full of various dreams with a common theme of being warned. He would wake up absolutely drenched in sweat. Still, he said nothing to his wife.

The birthing day finally arrived, and it was time to go to the hospital. After already having three children, the procedure for delivery was well-known and familiar to them. Early on they had made arrangements so Jimmy could be in the delivery room. After only about twenty minutes of labor, their fourth boy came into the world—but something was dreadfully wrong. Their baby was born dead.

Everyone was stunned by the shocking reality of something that could not be real but was. The doctor was so upset and couldn't even look up. The nurse turned and walked out of the delivery room. It was all beyond anyone's comprehension.

The next few days were incredibly difficult. As grief set in, it felt as if their rational world had turned upside down. Within a week Jimmy couldn't even work anymore. He had been working for a contractor as a carpenter, but he simply couldn't focus, had no energy, and just wanted to crawl into a hole. He eventually learned from the doctor that their little boy's death was caused by something very rare, but that it would be good in future pregnancies to have a test that would tell them the condition of the fetus in the womb.

Over time things leveled out and they even had another child—their first daughter—for a total of four children. They were able to get the medical test necessary and their daughter was perfectly normal. A few years later they were pregnant once more but didn't have the funds for the special test, which was extremely expensive. Besides, the odds were one in 500,000 that it would reoccur.

Imagine their shock as they went through a nearly identical experience as they had with their previous baby boy, except this time it was a girl and she lived for about an hour.

How do people move forward through this kind of unspeakable pain and loss? Jimmy would say he didn't, he couldn't move through it on his own. He knew they were *carried* through it.

One afternoon, he decided to go to his favorite creek and fish at the base of the fish ladder, just before it reached the hatchery. There was a protruding log he always stood on to cast against a granite wall, allowing his lure to drop into the water. And almost without exception he would catch a spawning steelhead trout.

Gathering up his catch, he began to climb the hill to his car, only to discover a large iridescent blue butterfly fluttering around at the top of the hill that settled on the antenna of his car. It was Henrietta, of course, which Jimmy knew for sure when he saw the telltale chunk missing from the edge of one wing. He dropped his fish and simply sat on the ground, suddenly acutely aware he had survived the loss of two of his children. And he was somehow okay. Henrietta was once more leaving an imprint of comfort and peace on his heart. And with that, she flew away.

Scene 16: Viola

The death of their second child happened after they had settled in the rural community of Viola Valley, Oregon. It was a delightful community perched in the hills south of Gresham. Initially, Jimmy was working for a local school district as a construction supervisor. They lived on a dead-end road at a 120-acre parcel available to them for a year while the owners were out of the country. The property included a large house, a stream, a pond, a sixteen-stall horse barn in need of much repair work, a corral, and an enclosed riding arena. The upper half the property was all forest timber.

Not far from their house was the small Viola Community Church, one of the first churches built in the Northwest, more than 150 years old with its original bell tower and bell. The walls did not consist of regular timbers. Instead the structure was made of boards going one direction diagonally nailed to boards perpendicularly. The nails were square, as they were hand-hammered by a blacksmith. This was discovered when the back end of the building was remodeled into an office.

One neighbor who was also a church member saw the condition of the barn Jimmy intended to repair and said, "Let's have a work party!" Before long there was a regular group of youth who came on Saturdays to help with the repairs. The second floor was intended for hay storage, but the floors had deteriorated and were unsafe. A local contractor donated lumber and in no time at all there was a floor longer than a full-sized basketball court. Naturally, they put up basketball hoops and the game was on! This morphed into the kids wanting to get together for special occasions and the "Red Barn Explosion" was born. They would play games, listen to music, and discuss the principles of the Word of God and how it applied to their lives.

This continued for several months until the owners of the property returned from their overseas trip.

Right around the time Jimmy and his family moved up the hill to a mobile home, he received a very unexpected offer. The Viola Community Church they attended had a pastor who was in seminary and was only around on Sundays. The church invited Jimmy to be their pastor. He was floored by this development, but also honored and excited. After all, Jimmy had wanted to be a pastor ever since he met and spent time with pastor John all those years ago, and in spite of his family's history with his father's inexplicably antagonistic stance toward Christianity.

During the next three years the church grew from just a dozen people to more than seventy-five families. Jimmy hadn't felt so alive in years. And then it all came crashing down around him. Rumors were flying that Jimmy had embezzled thousands of dollars from a friend of his named Donald. It wasn't true. This however created great confusion and turmoil for him personally.Jimmy felt he had no choice but to resign his pastorate. Unbeknownst to him, Donald had been spreading these rumors from the very moment Jimmy was invited to become the pastor. None of it was true, but Donald had left his deceptive fingerprints throughout the community.

But the damage was done and couldn't be undone. Jimmy lost his church, and it hit him hard. It was a truly crushing blow to let go of what had become the most deeply satisfying connection he'd ever had to the human race.

He fell into a deep depression and didn't even feel like going fishing, which had become one of his favorite pastimes. And yet he still found himself regularly sitting at the water's edge of some of his favorite fishing holes. Inevitably, tears would flow as the events of his life replayed themselves in his mind—all the feelings, the victories, the disappointments—flooded in, uncontrolled.

It was not uncommon during these emotional sojourns to feel a feathery fluttering on the back of his neck, after which Henrietta would appear on his left shoulder. On one such occasion, Jimmy wondered why she always came from behind, and why did she always settle on his left shoulder? No sooner did he consciously form this question than the answer came to him in a moment of revelation: She appeared when he was lost and trapped by the memories of things *left behind*, and she always "had his back."

Scene 17: The Affair

The residual pain left from resigning the church reverberated through not only Jimmy's family but also a college student who was staying with them at the time. Ten years younger than him, she was a breath of fresh air in the midst of a polluted environment. Her words were encouraging and always served as a means to distract him from his troubles. She too had a bad relationship with her father, and always referred to Jimmy as "Dad." They began spending more and more time together as their lives became increasingly intermeshed in a way that soon proved to be dangerous.

Within months they soon faced the fact they were being engulfed by their feelings for each other and found themselves on a precipice. They were in fact on the edge of making a decision about becoming intimate with one another. Their embraces soon became full-blown desire for each other. Something may start innocently, but the nature of self-deception allows each progressive stage to be rationalized away until the realization of having gone much too far comes far too late.

And so things progressed until one day they stood hand-in-hand before Jimmy's wife, Mary Jane, telling her they were going away for the weekend. Mary Jane said nothing, so they ventured down a road from which very few people return whole.

****

In the midst of year two of his ongoing affair with Karen, he and his family were living in Seattle, Washington. Karen was in Portland, Oregon. The affair served as a minimal distraction from the constant pain and heaviness that overshadowed him every day. Karen was always asking, "What's wrong?" but Jimmy could never provide any kind of real answer no matter how often she asked the question.

He was caught in the grips of a deep, dark depression and was barely surviving. He had driven down to Portland to have dinner with Karen but decided to cut their evening short and said he was going to get a motel for the night since it was late. She asked, "Do you want me to stay with you?"

Jimmy replied, "No, I'm just in a tough spot and need to be alone." They embraced with what felt like a final hug and he drove to the motel. Alone in his room, the next hour brought intense feelings of finality and an overwhelming sense that he couldn't go on like this.

He was incredibly thirsty and had a wicked headache. He went out to an all-night market near the motel where he gathered up a half a dozen cans of soda and went to the aisle where they had pain relievers with the intention of purchasing enough Tylenol to alleviate his headache. Without consciously thinking about it, he picked up three bottles of Extra Strength Tylenol, 200 tablets per bottle. Back in his room he sat quietly as he methodically opened the bottles of Tylenol and cans of soda, consuming all 600 tablets. He turned off the lights and closed his eyes. His world was quiet for the first time in a long while as the darkness of the night engulfed him.

About an hour later there was a knocking on his motel door. It was the husband of the family where Karen was staying. "Jimmy...Jimmy, it's Harold, Are you okay?" Karen had told him of her concern that Jimmy was not in a good place and she was afraid for him.

By default, Jimmy got up and answered the door. Jimmy decided there was no way he was going to admit to Harold what he had done. But one glance in the wastebasket next to his bed revealed the empty containers of Extra Strength Tylenol. He just looked at Jimmy and said, "What do you want me to do?"

Jimmy replied, "I don't know, and I really don't care."

Harold asked, "Will you let me help you?" Jimmy nodded his head and Harold immediately set about taking Jimmy to his car. He was a physician's assistant at a local hospital and they simply walked into the Emergency room and found an empty bay. Harold gave him glass after glass of activated charcoal solution to induce vomiting. That went on for about four hours and Jimmy was transferred to a room that served as a 72-hour hold for patients who had tried to commit suicide. Turns out the Tylenol itself wouldn't have killed Jimmy, but it would have wrecked his liver, which in turn would have killed him in a slow painful death!

Within about a week it was determined there was no liver damage at all, which was quite amazing based on how much Tylenol he took. Very little of it had a chance to break down and enter his bloodstream.

While he was in the hospital, there was a constant flow of visitors from his previous congregation. Jimmy found himself back in his pastoral role of caring for people, in spite of why he was in the hospital himself. The only exception was an older couple who visited and simply sat with him, saying nothing at all. Their visit was a breath of fresh air!

Mary Jane flew down from Seattle and when it was time to go home, they drove back together. Karen did not visit, though it wasn't long before the affair was back on. They always seemed to gravitate back to one another.

What Jimmy didn't know until after this incident was how he came from a paternal family wherein almost every male head of the household for six generations had either committed or attempted suicide. From the hanging of his father's father in the basement of the Lutheran Church where he was an Elder, all the way back to drownings and self-inflicted gunshot wounds in the 1700s. Some survived but were debilitated for life, confined to wheelchairs or mental institutions. This began a quest Jimmy and his wife committed to: This trend is going to stop with this generation. He spoke at length with their children, particularly the three boys.

The next few months consisted of trying to bring some semblance of order to his world. Not far from where they lived was a beautiful country hillside with a favorite oak tree he often visited, as it overlooked the valley. One afternoon as he was sitting at the base of the tree with his knees pulled up to his chest, Henrietta suddenly landed on his left knee. He carefully extended his index finger and she perched herself right in front of him.

The next few minutes were like being caught in a time-warp and life stopped. There was an absolute stillness between the two of them. Jimmy returned Henrietta to his left knee and closed his eyes, falling asleep. When he awoke, he was full of an inner sense that in spite of everything that had happened, he was going to now be able to move forward.

****

The on-and-off affair went on for a total of three years. Even when one or the other moved to a different state, they always ended up reconnecting. Finally one night Jimmy told Mary Jane he was going to leave her for good, which had them both in tears, though for different reasons. Ultimately, however, Jimmy realized he couldn't do that to his children. The unspoken implication was he could apparently do exactly that to his wife.

Having resolved to stick with his family, Jimmy then faced the daunting task of disentangling himself from the mess he'd made. He told his illicit partner one night it was over because he could not abandon his family. Her unexpected response was that she understood and would be perfectly happy if they only saw each as infrequently as once a month. Jimmy's intention to bring the affair to a conclusion seemed to only present an opportunity to keep it going.

After several more months of this, Jimmy again reached a point where he needed it to stop. During a Saturday visit with her, he once again declared it was over between them. And this time it appeared to sink in, though it left him feeling like he had literally just killed her.

****

One afternoon while driving around trying to make sense of his life, his car broke down. As he waited for a tow truck, he sat on the road many miles north of where he lived. A huge wave of guilt was washing over him. He felt guilty for letting down his church by resigning. He felt immense guilt for what he had put his wife and family through with the affair. But most of all he felt guilty about the person he had become. There were no tears, just the heavy weight of guilt.

In that moment he suddenly felt the familiar feathery fluttering at the base of his neck, and sure enough there was Henrietta on his left shoulder. And although he felt an immediate sense of peace and comfort, it would be many years before he could truly forgive himself.

Scene 18: Paralysis

Several years passed and Karen moved to Spokane, Washington, and married. Jimmy heard she had a little girl. Jimmy and Mary Jane never spoke of the affair. Their focus was on their children, and Jimmy's successful career as a remodeling contractor. Although it looked like he had moved on from Karen, it didn't feel that way inside.

It was a Monday morning and Jimmy had made arrangements to go down south to begin a remodel on a barber shop. It was for a long-term client of many years and today was demolition day. He got up early but was not feeling good and called Fred to ask if he could come at noon, as it would only take about four hours to dismantle everything. Jimmy went back to sleep. He woke up a couple hours later and collapsed in the bathroom, white as a sheet.

Mary Jane saw him having a seizure and called 9-1-1. The paramedics arrived and transported him to the local hospital in Kirkland. Slowly Jimmy became conscious once more of his surroundings. He could talk, but the rest of his body was not working. After tests and evaluations it was determined Jimmy was a quadriplegic, paralyzed from the neck down. He was transferred to a private room where the family could come to visit.

There were many hours he was by himself, apart from the physical therapist trying to keep his muscles from atrophying due to lack of movement, the volunteers who came in to feed him, and the nurses who helped him with elimination. In those quiet alone times, he found himself continually thinking about his father.

The next several months consisted of multiple types of tests to determine why he was paralyzed. Every other day he was in physical therapy. Over the next two years things progressed very slowly from wheelchairs to walkers, then to quad canes as he returned home.

This new phase of life was challenging on many levels. His self-worth was found in what he could do and how well he could do it. There was a long period of time figuring out who he was outside of what he did, since he couldn't do much of anything except talk.

As his range of motion was gradually restored, he realized he was experiencing dissociative episodes of lost time. He thought these lasted only a few minutes, but his family told him it more often lasted days at a time. After nine hospitalizations and nine widely divergent diagnoses, he was at a standstill.

During one hospitalization, his head was shaved after a CT scan as he awaited a specialist to perform brain surgery. The surgeon positioned Jimmy differently with his head back and mouth open to take a final set of pictures and said, "Wow! I have great news! Except for now being bald, you don't need surgery." For Jimmy it was *not* great news because it meant he was back to square one with no resolution to his condition.

Honestly, no one knew why Jimmy was paralyzed. Then one day he was in a Social Security Disability hearing and the state called the last neurologist he had seen. This neurologist had a different diagnosis than all the other medical professionals he'd seen. The neurologist said he believed Jimmy was suffering from a traumatic event from which his body had dissociated and to which it was now trying to reconnect. He called it a Conversion Disorder in which the body moves into dysfunction as the mind converts it from having been connected to a trauma.

Scene 19: Facing the Dragon

It was a typical October morning in Seattle as Jimmy made his way to his regular 10:00 am appointment with the psychotherapist he'd been seeing for two years in order to sort out his increasingly difficult emotional life.

The morning dew over Mercer Island was particularly thick and heavy so close to the famous Seattle Harbor waterfront, "The Bay at the Sea." He arrived to his appointment and parked close to the elevator that would take him to the thirteenth floor. Stepping into the elevator, Jimmy wished he had cancelled that day's session; his feelings were as impenetrable as the fog that followed him. But he had made a commitment to his therapist, "Kathy the Queen," that he would always show up, barring his death.

He had spent the previous week in Hawaii at a private home perched on an oceanside cliff with amazing views of the crashing sea that filled his senses with awe. Such an experience might so captivate a person's wellbeing that they would be caught up in the moment, not wanting to leave. But for Jimmy, the opposite was true. There was an overwhelming restlessness to his every waking and slumbering moment.

Ding—the elevator bell indicated it had reached the thirteenth floor. Jimmy drew in a deep breath and prepared for yet another visit with his therapist. He couldn't help but wonder why he kept coming when two years of sessions seemed to be going nowhere.

But prior to their first visit she had read through the large box of medical files he had sent to her, accompanied with a note that read: *After you have read the contents, my medical records from nine hospital stays, call me if you think you can help me*. She did call, and they agreed to work together – and to keep working together in order to "Face the Dragon," whatever it might be.

Kathy's fee was $145.00 per hour, but Jimmy and his family were dirt-poor at that point and on welfare. They had given up their pets as they could not afford pet food. Christmas presents for their children that year were all provided by their landlord. At the end of their initial consultation, Jimmy stood up, shook Kathy's hand, and said, "I'll see you next week, same time same place." Kathy reinforced it was important to his process that he have "skin in the game" financially and that she needed to charge him. He totally agreed, but how would he ever be able to pay?

"So, Jimmy," Kathy said in her soft demeanor, "That will be seven dollars a week until we are done, do you understand?" Only after Jimmy had agreed and was halfway down to the bottom floor did he realize the magnitude of what had taken place. He went back up to her office and expressed his gratitude. She smiled and reminded him that he needed to keep up his end of the agreement. Every week it was an assortment of change and dollar bills that found their way to the appointment, and every week Kathy would simply put the stipend in a large jar.

Jimmy reached into the right pocket of his jacket to gather up his due diligence for this day's appointment. The chair in which he sat waiting for his appointment was positioned beneath some shelves he had built to hold puzzles made available to clients. The shelves were Jimmy's small way of saying thank you.

The Shelves Beneath
Perfect I'm not, look closely and see
But hope I've found despite the appearance of
what was once me...
See, I consist of that which normally is discarded,
having lines skewed, rough, and badly departed.
With loving patience that's purposed, I've been embraced,

'til I've come to appreciate my journey,
the path from disgrace.
I thought I would have needed new parts,
a replacement to live, a bypass
to accomplish the way of my heart,
But now I know as I look back,
I can see it's truly just me, aligned in Harmony.
If I, without soul and spirit, can have a sense of order
from that which I've come,
then you who have read my legacy must know,
that life is yours to own and cherish
as you express the emblems of your character,
the lamp post of your heart!

The office door opened to reveal Kathy, a slight person of five-feet-two-inches with long flowing brown hair that bounced as she walked. Her dress was always pristine and colorful—a reflection of her personality. Kathy went to sit in her usual upholstered armchair and Jimmy chose where he would sit among the other assorted chairs scattered about the room. The light was dim. One small ray of sunlight found its way traversing along the carpet, setting a boundary down the center. Jimmy chose the chair closest to Kathy with the light behind him.

They spent the next few moments catching up as usual. Kathy never really seemed to have an agenda, at least not one that was obvious. She simply made herself present to the moment. Jimmy was restless and found himself gazing out the window rather than making eye contact as he usually did. Kathy, while waiting for him to connect, reached to the round table at her side and picked up her keys. She simply held them loosely in her fingers and making a soft tingling sound.

Jimmy was now focusing his gaze back towards Kathy and saw among keys a small tube. It was about three inches long with a diameter about the same as her index finger. It contained a thick, clear fluid like glycerin in which floated an assortment of stars, squares, and various other shapes, all of which were different reflective colors. It created a cascading effect as activated by the movement of her wrist. The mesmerizing movement of the reflective shapes somehow triggered a shift in time and space.

Jimmy was now seven years old. He was outside playing with his dad's dog, Laddie. After playing fetch and straying ever further from the house, Laddie suddenly decided he'd had enough and returned home. Jimmy was feeling more adventurous, drawn by the fragrance of the Eucalyptus trees that lined the rim of the canyon at the end of their street.

He could hear his mother's voice in his head saying he was never to venture near there without proper supervision. But he was thinking how acquiring fresh Eucalyptus leaves would be a great treat for his recently acquired friend, a turtle he named Rusty because of the brown streaks on his portable home. He knew younger trees produced the best diet for his friend, so he was looking for shorter trees with bright green leaves, signifying they were newly grown and tender. He peered over the edge of the canyon and saw many short trees just below where he stood. Looking about he determined the best and safest route to get there. The floor of the canyon was covered with a blanket of old leaves that resounded with a distinct crunch as he walked.

Suddenly, he could hear muffled sounds just ahead of him. The hair on his little arms stood straight up and he got goose bumps all over. He was feeling sick. To console himself he took off the small backpack he was wearing that contained his best friend in the world, Poopeatto—a skinny and very worn brown spider monkey puppet.

As Jimmy moved closer to the sounds, he found himself behind a thick bush, about twice his height, through which he could see the figure of a person hunched over something on the ground. It was a man and an undressed body lying flat on the ground—a woman who was clearly in distress. The man was lying on top of her and covering her mouth with his hands as he moved back and forth. She then must have bit him as he let out a violent yell and declared he was going to kill her. He drew a knife from his belt and stabbed the woman over and over until she moved no longer.

Frozen in terror, Jimmy's heart was pounding so hard in his chest he was sure the man could hear it. He broke out in a sweat and began to shake uncontrollably. His bowels turned to water, gushing out with the force of a hose. At the very moment Jimmy thought his entire body would explode, without warning, a peaceful calm settled over him. A new reality descended upon him like a comforting blanket—a reality in which he did not see what he just saw.

The man wiped the knife off and returned it to his belt. He then reached into his jacket pocket for cigarettes and sat quietly as he smoked two. The smell of cigarettes were forever imprinted in Jimmy's mind at that moment as something he hated. Afterwards, the man picked up his jacket, swung it over his right shoulder, and walked right past Jimmy hidden behind the bush. Jimmy waited to be sure the man was really gone, then crawled over to the bloody body and covered her with dry eucalyptus leaves. A breeze penetrated the scent of warm blood, dissipating the odor.

Jimmy picked himself up and began to walk out of the canyon when he realized he did not have his best friend in the world, his monkey puppet Poopeatto. He began to cry softly and when he got home, his mother eventually saw how he seemed distressed and asked him what was wrong. He began to stutter and eventually said he had lost Poopeatto up by the store, behind a big truck with lots of wheels. Over the next three days, countless hours were spent searching for Poopeatto, to no avail. Jimmy didn't speak much for a long time after that.

This fateful session with his therapist was the one that brought back to fore the trauma he had experienced at the tender age of seven. The one neurologist who had diagnosed him with Conversion Disorder was correct. After forty years, Jimmy finally came face to face with his dragon.

Scene 20: The Divorce

Jimmy's now tenth hospitalization over two years became his last. The week before being discharged he had a visitor. He wasn't in his room at the time, so they left a note.

The visitor was a man who saw the same therapist he'd been seeing and was a member of a support group Jimmy attended. The note simply said, "If there is any way we can be of help let us know." The "we" aspect meant his wife had been with him.

It was mid-afternoon and Jimmy was waiting for his wife, Mary Jane, to show up to take him home from his stay in the hospital. It was nineteen days before Christmas, and this had certainly been the strangest Christmas season he had ever experienced. When they arrived home, no one else was there and Mary Jane said, "I need to talk to you about one of our children." She went on to say a counselor came by yesterday and left her card.

You see, one of their children had been seeing a counselor with someone that past year and Jimmy thought it was that person that had come by. Mary Jane went on to say that an incident had been reported to Children's Protective Services (CPS) of something that supposedly had taken place six years prior in their household.

The card was not from the person who was counseling their child, but was from CPS, worker and within the next twenty-four hours either Jimmy needed to leave the home or the child would need to leave. Mary Jane asked him, "What are we to do?"

To them it was obvious the child couldn't leave the home, being only thirteen years old, so it seemed there was really no decision to be made. Mary Jane explained there had to be a separation until the investigation was complete. Jimmy obviously decided he would be the one to leave, but his wife reminded him he had just gotten out of the hospital. Where would he go and how would he take care of himself?

Jimmy took a deep breath and said, "In the more than thirty years you have known me, is there anything about me that would make you think I could be abusive to anyone, let alone our own child?"

She responded, "Of course not!"

The allegation was more than impossible and wrong—it was ridiculous! In the past, for nine years they had served as house parents for seven to ten children who had been abused. But it did bring back memories of when he was a pastor at Viola Community Church and Donald had accused him of embezzling thousands of dollars from him. How could people make such false accusations that couldn't be further away from the truth?

In the Viola situation, Jimmy had worked for free while Donald was overseas. He took care of spec homes Donald had built to sell. Jimmy handled the sales and warrantee issues, taking only $200 from each sale, even though he worked extra hours each day to deal with problem after problem due to poor construction and Donald's unwillingness to be a good steward of his financial commitments.

That's why the elder of the church had dismissed Donald's allegations. The people in the church were also totally aware of what Jimmy was doing in relation to the properties. Jimmy had kept detailed ledgers. But Donald was such a dear friend that the whole thing became so emotionally jarring and threw Jimmy's perception of reality so far off that he felt like he had to resign from the church.

In this new situation with his child, the allegations were again devastating in spite of being completely untrue. One lasting impact is that three of Jimmy's now five children haven't spoken to their father in more than twenty years.

Jimmy gathered up a few things, went to his truck, turned the key, and began to drive away. But to where? He was stunned. How could any of this be real? Jimmy remembered he had a county human services resource pamphlet tucked away somewhere. Finding it, he made a phone call and was given three days of emergency housing.

After those three days, he managed to find another place where he could stay for a week. It was a group house in which he had a separate bedroom with a mattress on the floor. Among the others in the house was a young girl who had a cat by the name of JR, for Junior. This was ironic because he was twenty-eight pounds and wore bells around his neck—he was a predator and killed anything that moved, especially rabbits. The bells warned potential prey of his presence. He was anything but a Junior.

Within a day JR was coming into his room and laying on Jimmy's chest at night. Jimmy couldn't ever seem to sleep. He'd try to hold back tears but always resulting in sobbing most the night. JR's owner was headed off to jail for six months (drug possession charge) and asked Jimmy to look after JR. She was surprised because JR hated men and always ran from them. But it looked like JR had picked Jimmy, and the cat quickly became his lifeline.

Jimmy was a day away from having to leave the house. His temporary assistance for food and gasoline was also ending. It was Thursday and time for his regular support group therapy session. He hoped to see the man who had left him a note in the hospital because he sure needed to figure some things out right now. But the man wasn't at the meeting. He was a commercial airline pilot and sometimes his work schedule simply didn't allow him to attend.

After the meeting, Jimmy was leaving and ran into the man, who said, "I don't know why I came, since the meeting is over!" They ended up going to the local Denny's restaurant and had a long conversation. Jimmy realized for the first time in his life he was asking for help. It was a huge moment for him as he was so used to being the helper and not the one needing help! He had always gone through everything seemingly alone, except for the occasional visit from Henrietta, whose presence always brought him immense comfort.

Jimmy began to explain he needed a place to stay. The man said, "Can you come by tomorrow and meet my wife? She has three favorite canaries, so we have to see if JR will work." The canaries were a gift from her mother, who had recently passed away.

Jimmy said, "I only need a place to stay for a little while." He couldn't—he wouldn't—give up JR, so there was a lot at stake the next day when the two of them set out to meet with the man and his wife. The home was on the shore of a beautiful lake which was ever so peaceful. It was a large home where they had raised all four of their children. There was plenty of room for Jimmy and JR.

Jimmy was holding JR as they entered the house and walked into the family room where the couple was sitting with the canaries. JR's eyes got very large with anticipation and Jimmy simply took his index finger, thumped JR's nose firmly, and in an instructive manner clearly said, "No!" After two more times JR got it, and never looked at those canaries again. As far as he was concerned, they didn't even exist.

JR and Jimmy lived in a room on the second floor that had a window just above the roofline. In the morning JR would jump out on the roof, go over to the Pergola and jump down, about a ten-foot drop, and land with a pronounced *thump*, and everyone used to say, "Well, JR is up!"

This new residence was more than a place to stay, since it became a place where his heart was embraced by other people, in a way that only one human being can do with another, which is the essence of healing.

Soon Jimmy contacted the detectives and went in and voluntarily did a lie detector test. He was told it would be a while before they were able to interview all of his neighbors and anyone else they could contact who knew him before, so they could make a decision. Nine months went by and he heard nothing.

Finally, he called to tell the head detective he was moving out of state and wanted to know the disposition of the case, since he didn't want to be seen as fleeing and bring on another problem. The head detective said the case was closed. She had finished her investigation and he could go home. The only problem was, there was no home to go to.

Mary Jane had received counsel from different people who convinced her the allegations must be true, as her child had never lied before. Jimmy was of the opinion the child did believe it was true, even though it wasn't. He eventually realized his only recourse was to let go of his relationship with his wife, as he could do nothing to influence her decisions, nor did he want to.

Jimmy ultimately got a job at an all-night market since he wasn't sleeping at night anyway. And eventually there was a semblance of order which brought him to a point where he needed to determine how he was going to move on. During this time, he had been in contact with his mom, who lived in San Diego. She continually told him he could move there as she had plenty of room in her house. After they moved in, she fell immediately in love with JR, who stayed with her until he died.

Jimmy had no desire to return to construction work, but a spark ignited inside him when he learned about vocational rehabilitation. He applied at the California Rehab organization when he discovered they would pay for his further education. He soon enrolled in a school full-time. Four years later, he finished school and spent another year as a student teacher, per his agreement with the school.

By that time it was clear his marriage was over, but he was still married. His mother commented she had seen a newspaper ad that said, "Get a divorce for $50." He remembered how Kathy, his therapist, had said years previously after meeting with Mary Jane a couple of times, "Jimmy, she will never make her mind up," which was very true. "You will have to initiate a divorce when it's time." Jimmy went through the process, put together the necessary information to initiate a divorce decree and filed it with the San Diego Municipal Court.

He mailed the paperwork to Mary Jane and about three weeks later got a brown legal envelop from an attorney in Seattle, which she had retained to represent herself in response to what she had received from him. It simply re-stated the same information Jimmy had filed and made him the recipient and Mary Jane the plaintiff. Jimmy called the attorney and asked what he was to do now. The attorney said he didn't need to do anything, that this was the completed divorce. Jimmy said, "Thank you," and hung up.

That afternoon was full of mixed emotions that left him numb. But what he held in his hands was a declaration to move forward.

Scene 21: A Ghost from the Past

A lot happened in the decade after Jimmy remembered witnessing the murder—moving to San Diego, the divorce, completing school. He eventually remarried and was in the process of opening a private practice in Carlsbad. One

Thursday morning he was on his way to the local hospital with his therapy dog, Sounder, to meet patients in the brand-new cardiology clinic. He usually went to this hospital on Tuesdays, but he wanted to be there for the Thursday opening of the clinic.

Driving along around 8:30 AM, they came to a stop sign where Jimmy noticed a familiar oncoming car. It was the woman from across the street where he lived coming home after dropping off her seven-year-old son at school. But all Jimmy could see were her eyes. It was as if there were no other aspects to her person except her eyes. *That's strange*, Jimmy thought to himself.

After an hour spent at the hospital, Jimmy and Sounder returned home. When they were within a block of their house there was a police car blocking the road. Jimmy drove around to the other entrances into their housing development, but they were blocked by police cars as well. A lot of yellow crime tape was stretched across the streets.

Finding a place to park nearby, Jimmy hoped they could just walk home. An officer met him and began to explain that there had been a crime and it was an active crime scene, which meant no one was allowed in until they finished their investigation. It turned out he couldn't access his home for a couple of days. Fortunately Jimmy had his dog, contacted his wife, and made arrangements for a place to stay.

When they got to the hotel room they turned on the television and saw the story. A woman was found dead in her home. It appeared she had been raped and stabbed multiple times. It was the woman he had noticed when driving to the hospital earlier in the day.

The crime scene was gruesome. She had been stabbed with a knife multiple times, but also with a pair of pruning shears from the garage. It appeared she had also been tasered several times. All the while had struggled, fought back, screaming for help.

It didn't take long before Jimmy began feeling a heavy sense of guilt. Normally, he was probably the only adult in the neighborhood who was around during the day. And he would have been home had he not changed which day he went to the hospital that week. Maybe he would have heard her cries for help. Maybe he could have prevented her grisly death. The murderer was apprehended immediately as he was leaving the property. Jimmy, as it turned out, was the last person other than the killer to see his neighbor alive.

A couple days later, the husband showed up to visit Jimmy. There just weren't words, only heartfelt embraces and tears. Finally permitted to go back, his neighbor went home. Jimmy watched as he came out of his house with the set of knives from the kitchen and threw them away.

There was a fund available for victims of such a crime to cover the cost of a company to clean the home, but the husband did not accept the assistance. He was part of a rugby team from Johannesburg, South Africa, and the only people he wanted in his home were those friends. They were all part of a construction company and well-qualified to assist, both emotionally and physically. The next morning his buddies showed up in their trucks and Jimmy knew the guy in charge. He walked across the street and asked if he could help.

The front door was replaced and stained, as well as the security screen. Banister rails were missing, chunks of the hardwood floor had been cut out downstairs as well as carpet pieces from upstairs, all taken as evidence by the police for use during the trial. Windows were broken and screens torn. There were blood stains throughout the house, the floors, the bathroom walls, doorknobs, light switches, kitchen sinks, and tile. It was horrifying to see how prolonged and extended the struggle had been.

Jimmy put his extensive carpenter and electrician skills to good use over the next several days. He could see the man's friends and the construction foreman struggling with the sheer volume of evidence the murderer left behind. It was trauma unlike anything any of them had ever before seen. Jimmy, however, remained calm and undistracted by any of it, and the construction foreman noticed and commented on it. In the face of such trauma, Jimmy simply dissociated from it. And while his "ability" to do so was useful in his work with trauma victims that allowed him to maintain positive focus, psychological disassociation is not a healthy way to deal with trauma—it was a form of denial. If you don't face the dragon, it will eventually burst forth from within you to wreak all kinds of havoc in your life.

Jimmy and his wife were scheduled to leave in a couple of days on a flight to Seattle to participate in a three-day conference. Immediately after helping finish the project, they left for Seattle and the hotel where the conference was being held. They went to the initial opening ceremonies, then returned to their room during a break. Jimmy's wife looked at him and said, "What's wrong?"

Jimmy didn't have an answer. He didn't know what was wrong, but all of a sudden his world had turned upside down. He exclaimed, "I can't do this..." With nothing else spoken, his wife understood he was in a very difficult place.

For the next couple days she attended the conference while Jimmy just walked and walked and walked. The hotel was right on Highway 99 and Jimmy surely walked at least forty miles up and down that road, even in the pouring rain. back and forth, up one side of the road and down the other. At first he felt like he was lost in time, but then realized he was *stuck* in time—as a seven-year-old boy witnessing a murder as horrible as the one he had just helped erase from his neighbor's home.

On his wanderings, Jimmy sorted through his feelings and what was happening to him. He realized healing would itself be a life-long journey. He could try to convince himself he had moved on in life. He had gone to school, remarried, and even started a new business. But here he was, once again debilitated by the echoes of a long-ago trauma, triggered anew by a more recent trauma that touched his life deeply.

With the awareness that this was going to take a long time, Jimmy realized he had a choice to make. He could choose to be a victim, or he could choose to learn from his experiences, share his journey, and help others on their own journey to heal from the grip of trauma. Would he choose to be a victim or a healer? As he contemplated this choice, the rainclouds parted and warm, wonderful sunshine streamed down upon him. And then he felt something he hadn't felt for quite a long time—a feathery fluttering at the back of his neck, and out of the corner of his eye saw a large iridescent blue butterfly with a chunk missing from one wing settle gracefully on his shoulder. He smiled at his old friend and made his choice.

ACT III
REFLECTIONS

NOTE TO READER:
The following scenes are from the author's perspective.

Scene 22: Instinct

One of the themes of Jimmy's life was a deep interest in and appreciation for nature. Everything he encountered in his wilderness adventures filled him with awe and wonder. And this theme carried on throughout his life. He loved the ocean and was forever fascinated by waves breaking upon a shore. It always served as an instant gateway to consider the vastness and complexity of creation. In fact, it never occurred to him that nature in all its glory could be anything but designed by intent and infused with purpose.

Consider the kingdoms and categories of animals, plants, the environment, and the total universe. One can only pause in amazement of it all. Everything works like clockwork—*instinctually*, if you will. But this begs an important question: If all of created nature responds out of a predetermined purpose, with built-in direction or instinct, where does that leave the most peculiar creature of all—people? If a Creator set everything in motion with exactness, surely we human beings must also fall within that framework. And if the world we know operates from instinct by the Creator, then what is the instinctive response of people to their Creator?

Ah, but of course you're thinking human beings have free will, agency, and choice. After all, is this not what sets us apart from the rest of creation? Yes, of course, but what if it's only in the sense that we can think and reflect upon these differences and our own agency and free will. It doesn't mean we've been left out of the Creator's design of instinctive response. In fact, it's perfectly logical that it is only within our own agency as people we can choose to see or discover the instinctive response inherent to being human, and this instinctive response coincides with the Creator's purpose in creating us.

There are literally millions of examples that bring amazing, unique clarity to the process of how nature and its creatures are orchestrated with responses designed just for them. Multiply that by infinity, if you will, and you have an immense documentation of the DNA of the creation. Consider just one such story—the albatross and its migration flight.

On Kauai, the oldest of the Hawaiian Islands, there are 200-foot cliffs that serve as a nesting site for albatrosses. To get here, to this exact location, they fly more than 2,000 miles from the Alaskan coast. Upon arrival, they find a lifetime mate. After mating, they go about gathering pine needles for their nest, in which a single egg is laid. They take shifts sitting on the egg to keep it warm. The chick hatches within a couple of months, and the task of providing nourishment begins for the new member of the family. While one parent stays with the chick, the other one flies at least 1,500 miles one way to find squid in the ice cold arctic waters off the Alaskan shore. After about three days they have consumed enough squid to return back to Kauai. This particular diet is the only thing the new chick eats, as it consumes a regurgitated mixture of seawater and squid from the parent. This task goes on and on for several months!

Then begins the process of teaching the chick to be on its own and fly, and to acquire its own nourishment. This is called *fledging* and is quite hilarious to observe. One would think the nourishment they were receiving from their parents had a high alcoholic content as they tend to stumble and fall as they begin to spread their seven-foot wingspan. Time is spent over the next six to seven years as they mature in Alaska and then they continue this migration to their breeding grounds from Alaska to Kauai. The albatross is merely behaving by instinct, doing what it's meant to do, what it was designed and created to do. It's so wonderfully unique and specific to the albatross. Just thinking of it sets one's mind to soaring as high as the albatross itself in its migration flight with wonderment at the diversity and complexity of the creation we inhabit.

What, then, of human beings? There are forward-thinking people who invent things like electricity, cars, planes, phones, computers, and so on. There are people who work hard and provide courageously for their families. And there are also people who are stuck. Their "was" is their "is" and they can't seem to break from a debilitating cycle of disorder and *dysfunction*. And from this come all the support groups, mental institutions, correctional facilities, and so on to deal with those people. These are but a few of many types of people that make up the human race.

At first glance humans seem strikingly different from the rest of creation, for there seems to be no common pattern of being human the way there is a common pattern of being an albatross. And yet, looking deeper into the dichotomy of being human in the pages that follow, perhaps something will emerge that surprises you!

Scene 23: Companionship's Comfort—A Dog's Heart

Unique relationships between humans and animals have occurred throughout history, but few have a history as long and intertwined as the relationship between people and dogs. There is evidence of this relationship dating back many thousands of years, and more than 10,000 years before horses were domesticated.

In the Czech Republic a dog was found buried with a bone carefully placed in its mouth. This dog is believed to date back 32,000 years, and the bone is from a woolly mammoth. In Germany the skeleton of a disabled dog was found buried with a man and woman, dating back 14,300 years. And there's the mummified black dog of Tumat in Russia that dates back 12,450 years. Dogs were even deified in some ancient cultures, such as Anubis in Egypt, Xolotl for the Mayans, and Cerberus for the Greeks. These canine deities were believed to serve as guides, showing deceased people the way to the afterlife, or as guards of the next world.

On a talk radio program I was listening to one day, I heard the story of a man who died without any immediate family. Arrangements were made to have his remains transported two states away to be buried near his mother's gravesite. Interestingly, the man had a dog, but no one knew this. And yet, thirty-one days later, there was a dog found resting on the man's gravesite. It was the man's pet, and the only remaining evidence that the man had ever existed in this world.

When the story was published in the local paper about what the dog was doing, people began bringing him food and water. That continued for three years until the dog died on the man's gravesite. Over those years there was a disabled veteran who used to visit that cemetery and always spent time with the dog he found there. This veteran made arrangements for the dog to be buried next to his master. Master Sergeant Henry Jones realized how very comforting the time with the dog was for him, not realizing he had bonded so deeply until the dog was buried. He started making phone calls and put together one of the first organizations to pair veterans with a companion animal—and to this day it is one of the most vibrant forms of therapy used by the armed services.

There is actually a movie, Kochi, depicting a true story about an Alaskan Malamute that bonded with a businessman in Japan. Kochi accompanied his master to the train station every day. When the train returned at the end of the day, Kochi would be there wagging his tail to greet his master as he stepped off the train. There was an incident of some sort in which the man died, but Kochi continued for many years to greet the train, until one year he died in the snow, waiting for his master's return. For years, the local vendors around the train station cared for him and he loved the hot dogs they gave him.

I have my own experiences with three different dogs. As a child, my dad had a dog by the name of Patches, a black and white mut who was my best friend and constant companion. I didn't like to talk with people much, but I had many long conversations with Patches. He would look right at me, perk up his ears, and attend to everything I said while all the time wagging his tail.

As an adult having remarried, I made arrangements with my sister to remodel her kitchen in exchange for a puppy. She was a breeder of Whippets and Saint Bernards. She also had a friend who bred champion Golden Retrievers and we opted for one of those puppies in exchange for the remodel work. Sounder, known in American Kennel Club (AKC) circles as The Sound of Music, became the new addition to our family of two.

I was constantly astonished by the way Sounder would interact with people. My wife and I have a healthcare business and we have clients who come to see us. Sounder had an old milk crate with assorted toys in it, and somehow he decided certain clients should have certain toys. As someone would approach the entrance, Sounder would ascertain who it was, run across the room to his milk crate, ravage through it, and find a specific toy. He would then be at the door with the toy in his mouth and whining with his tail wagging. Each person who was a regular got the same toy every time they came.

A client mentioned to me one day he thought Sounder would make a wonderful therapy dog to visit people in the hospital. Sounder and I took a class to get certified and we became a Pet Therapy Team for our local hospital. We worked specifically in the Rehabilitation Ward. I was continually amazed how he interacted with patients with all types of needs, as if he had somehow received training for each specific type of situation.

One day while we were visiting, the charge nurse on the floor asked if we would visit a man who had recently come out of surgery. She explained his right arm and right leg had been amputated and he was having a difficult time. We were more than happy to oblige, and the patient gave his approval as well.

Usually when we visited people in their rooms, I would take a towel and drape it over the bed for Sounder to get up on it. But on this visit Sounder deviated from what he normally does. He went parallel to the man's bed and laid down on the floor at the head of the bed. The man allowed his left arm to fall from the bed and his fingertips somehow ended up exactly at Sounder's head. We were there for thirty minutes. The man never said a word and seemed to be in a trance. But he continually stroked Sounder's head with his fingers, which Sounder simply accepted. Sounder was giving more than receiving. As a tear rolled down the man's cheek, he quietly said, "Thank you," and in an instant Sounder got up and headed towards the door to leave.

The charge nurse had been watching the whole time and asked me as we left how in the world I trained my dog to do that. I said, "He's just being a dog." It was a profound lesson about the power of just being fully present.

As the years went on, I simply let Sounder do his thing. But it all came to an abrupt halt one morning when clients arrived at our office and he didn't get up.I immediately said to my wife, "Something is wrong with Sounder and I'm taking him to see the vet." The attendants brought a stainless steel cart and took him to the examination room. As I waited, I stepped outside and leaned against a planter. Another client was out there waiting for her dog as well. I had this wave come over me that I was going to lose my buddy and I began to cry. The lady standing next to me asked if she could give me a hug and said to me, "I am so sorry."

The vet came out and told me Sounder's stomach was distended because he was bleeding from his pancreas. He was full of cancer.

When I first came to the office, I was told that the doctor could only be there for a short while. We asked him to have Sounder put down because it was the only humane thing we could do. He stayed with us the entire afternoon until Sounder had passed. He also gave him a big hug. This was almost as difficult for him as it was for us because he had cared for Sounder since he was a puppy. He also had three Golden Retrievers of his own. It would be three years before I was ready for another dog.

****

One day I received a phone call from a client, asking if we would be willing to take care of their five-year-old child for a week while they went to a conference. It was quite an eventful week, to say the least. It had been a long time since I had been around a five-year-old. This was three years after Sounder had passed. The vet had made arrangements to have Sounder's ashes put in a small cedar box with a tiny little lock on it. One afternoon while sitting on the floor playing, the boy pointed to the box and asked, "What's that?"

How do you explain cremation to a five-year-old? There was a picture of Sounder from when he won first place at an AKC dog show. I began to explain to him how after the dog in the picture died, he was cremated and put in the box. Jonathan said, "Was he a little dog so he could fit in the box? And why is he locked in?" Well, somehow that brought humor to the whole thing in a way only children can do, and I don't know to this day if he knows what cremation is.

It was three years later at Christmas when I was finally ready to get another dog. I decided I was going to get a rescue dog and began a local search, but by the time we got there the dogs that interested me were gone. The day after Christmas I bravely did an internet search for rescue dogs locally. I say bravely because you have no idea how scary it is for me to do anything associated with computers. I declared to my wife I found a dog I wanted to see.

The puppy was at a rescue shelter located about a three-hour drive into the desert. I called the man who currently had the dog and asked if he wanted us to meet him at the rescue place. He said, "Our watchdog is kind of bipolar today and having a bad day. It would be best if we could meet at a different place." We arranged to meet at a mall where there was a pet shop. The man warned us, "He is very shy, hasn't been crated or in a car before, and he doesn't like men." I was feeling less and less confident about this whole trip.

When the man opened the crate, the puppy bounded out and came immediately to me. The man was very surprised by this since the puppy didn't want to have anything to do with him. I walked over to our car and the puppy followed. I opened the door to get something out of the car and he jumped right in!

Well, that says it all. It looks like he made his mind up and chose us. It was all rather fortuitus in hindsight. The man had been calling the puppy "Jack," but that didn't seem to fit him. The dog looks like he has a mask on, but Bandit didn't seem appropriate because we didn't want him to be a criminal canine. We decided to call him "Ranger," for the Lone Ranger.

Having gone through the pet therapy classes with Sounder, I realized all the things a pet therapy dog has to learn are perfect for any dog. So, from the very beginning I worked with Ranger to train him to be a therapy dog. I contacted my certifying organization and they simply gave me a date in order to have him evaluated. After evaluation the lady in charge said we have very few dogs that can be rated with what's called the Complex Rating, which simply meant there were no restrictions on who or how he visited. He received that rating because the woman said Ranger was clearly capable of handling himself appropriately in any situation.

That was just the beginning of Ranger's journey. We ended up doing volunteer work with a local hospice and bereavement center for children who have lost a loved one through death. We worked with children 3–7 years old and with the adults as well. Ranger is the camp dog for the bi-annual bereavement camp for children ages 7-18 years old who have lost a significant person to death. We also began to volunteer in trauma interventions with first responders when they had to deal with deaths, most of which were traumatic or violent. Our clients were the survivors of those situations.

On our social network page there is a picture of me holding him as a one-year-old puppy, which introduces us as a trauma intervention team. I currently work with people who are in their final stages of life from Alzheimer's, dementia, or stroke, which has provided many warm-hearted interactions of the two of us together with clients. My wife used to say, "I think you love the dog more than me!" My response used to be, "He's easier to get along with." Please note I say "used to."

Yes, there is something about the connection between the human heart and animals that is profound in ways words simply cannot adequately describe. There is an amazing comfort provided and actually shared between both. For me, it offers a unique way of being present to myself, particularly when things around me are stormy or difficult. There is something about the touch of physical connection between human and animal that transports me to a place where all the world stops, creating a profound appreciation of that specific moment in time.

One day when reflecting upon how we see ourselves, these words came bounding forth:

My Dog Doesn't Know that I am Ugly...

My dog doesn't know that I am ugly you see
because his sightfulness is contingent upon his
heart to me.

He somehow is absent from my failures and ambivalent
to my past,
having a simple focus and enjoying being on task.

I don't understand sometimes how he can be so detached
from reality.
while I am overwhelmed and heavy-laden with life,
he just wants to play with me.

When attempting to catch, he continually drops the ball.
He doesn't get down-hearted and upset,
he chooses to perceive it not as a fall.

Wagging away a smile, he goes for it again,
with the same enthusiasm as before,
comes he bounding home through the door.

My dog doesn't know that I am ugly you see,
he must have a different mirror than me.
He refuses to reflect on that which holds me back,
he is forever faithful, even when stretched forth
upon his mat.

What is there about the heart of a friend?
Can it really see me different than my spin?
Can it uphold me beyond my fears?
Dissipating the rhythm that comes with familiar tears?

My life has learned to find a respite that mends,
as it considers the heart of my four-footed friend.
Can the joy of life really be that way, living simply and
with purpose,

finding a difference in our day?

You know, I've come to understand
that as regularly as the tide washes in and out,
relationships are two-fold,
impacting those who are about.

I have a dog, his name is Fido,
I have raised him from a pup.
He can stand upon his back legs,
if you hold his front legs up.

WOOF!

Scene 24: A Spider's Web

It was just the other day, a bright and balmy summer afternoon. My dog, Ranger, and I were headed out the door to the back patio. He becomes quite animated with anything that moves, particularly if it flies. As soon as he was out the door, he was looking up in the air with attentive interest.

I looked up and there was a yellow butterfly suspended in one place and flapping its wings. I got a stepladder to investigate, discovered it was stuck in the web of a spider, and the spider was also aware of the butterfly's presence.

It was a large web spanning all the way from a tree to the eaves of our home, which meant the spider had quite a journey ahead to entrap what it had caught. Fortunately, the butterfly was on the outside edge of the spider's web.

Climbing to the top rung of the ladder, I could get a clear view of the web in its entirety. What an amazing work of art! It was planned with a geometric design and exactness that could only be achieved in our human world through CAD (computer aided design). I exclaimed to my wife I wanted to help release the butterfly from its forlorn future as the spider was on the move. The butterfly's legs were stuck on two silk threads. I was careful to aid the butterfly the best I could without causing injury and it was soon able to flutter off.

This experience left me with a thought: We members of the human race can aid, support, encourage, and hold accountable the people we have in our lives who are stuck or entrapped, if you will. Without some assistance, their future might remain a tangled-up mess. But what's unique to us, and not much different than Jimmy's friend Henrietta when she was a caterpillar, is how we create the entanglements that ensnare us. Henrietta purposely wrapped herself up, thread by thread, entrapping and encasing herself in a cocoon (although Jimmy always called them cocoons, the technical term of the sack for a butterfly is *chrysalis*, whereas cocoons are made by moths).

We, as human beings, through choice, word by word, action by action, thought by thought, create a fiber that over time will define our very being. In my office, there is a plaque hanging on the wall that says, *Our innermost dominant thought becomes our outmost tangible reality*.

Henrietta, after going through a metamorphosis (a dramatic change), she reached up, found a hole, tore her sack open, and unfolded herself into her new reality. And we as members of the human race must follow suit as well. We just have to find that hole, if you will, and tear away that which has bound us in order to find our new reality.

The only difference I can see is how we humans often embrace the reality we had before our entanglement, which I call our *was*. When our past is something we joyfully return to, then it is great when our *was* becomes our *is*. However, if our past is a depiction of dysfunction and pain and we never get away from it later on in life, then having our *was* as our *is* results in us being stuck and entangled. The record of the past plays over and over and over again. And every time you see one of these trapped people, you know what record is going to be playing because they're stuck. Not much different than the cocoon of the worm that wiggles and squirms as if trying to make sense of things. Personally, I have learned to be incredibly patient with stuck people. Rather than becoming irritated or frustrated by them, I see them as being on a path to freeing themselves, and maybe I can even help them on their journey to freedom.

I've seen people who have been entrapped for such a long period of time that they can't remember what it's like to feel normal, and it might be a surprisingly long time before they even have the desire or wherewithal to get unstuck. I've seen it in prisons, mental health wards, and support groups for people who are addicted, whether chemically or behaviorally.

Yet on the other end, we have those who are performers, though not necessarily in the theatre. These are people who are driven to succeed and are seen as very successful by most people. Jimmy was one of those people. He was a driven caretaker and was sensitive to everybody's needs and interacted with everybody's needs except the most obvious, his family at home. Desperate for more attention from his father, he once asked if he could make an appointment with him!

Hats off to the fathers who see their family as the most valuable aspect of their life. They know how to be present, to listen, to play, and interact in the family's process of growing. This thoughtfulness of heart then expands to embrace the community around them, their neighborhood, their workplace, their social community, but the foundation of it should be in the family. There is joy to be found in all our relationships with others.

Throughout much of 2020 the whole world was turned upside down by the novel coronavirus and COVID-19 global pandemic. Businesses were closed and children were not in school. Initially there was a blanket of fear and darkness that covered people's perceptions. But one afternoon, walking down our street with my dog, I noticed house after house where children were with their parents, either in the yard doing something, playing on scooters and skates, tie-dying t-shirts, and all kinds of other activities. This is not meant to downplay the seriousness of the pandemic and its far-reaching negative impacts. And yet, have there not been some silver linings along the way, such as rediscovering the joys of family life that should have been more present all along?

In Jimmy's case, he excelled at guiding and instructing others on how to relate better , and yet the wherewithal to actually do it himself in his own life eluded him most of the time. His father, after all, was the tree from which the apple (Jimmy) had fallen. From Jimmy's recollection, there were never conversations, just bellowing words projecting his father's displeasure that he wasn't perfect. Here's a poem that captures the sentiment:

If I'd Only Been a Tomato

I wish I was a tomato you see,
Because life would have seemed at least fairer to me.

I've found when my heart was so torn apart,
It caused me to question life, from the start

My hope cannot be found by what's in the past
Nor can it be reflected by the guilt I sense ever so fast.

My father was a man of integrity, I know
But compassion from him I knew not, by what he
could show.

His heart was so conflicted in life,
That he turned inward to handle his strife.

His manner was gruff, with a deliberance that stung,
While as a child I lived, with a shadow of what had
been hung.

When Christ along my path became King
I begin to realize the purpose for which my heart
would now sing.

The Song exclaimed itself ever so loud,
My existence seemed captured as if in a shroud.

There rose with a clatter, the noise of the past,
To destroy God's purpose as if it could last.

Loneliness found comfort through snakes, spiders, and
creatures of all kind,
In order to offset the need to connect, the human race,
which seemingly, I could not find.

As the years were spent by the need to belong, it
came clear
The paradox of a life that seemed to be caught in a
web of fear.

My father standing with rake in clear sight, His trusty
canine companion to tend, Eagerly engaged in the haven
of gardening delight, with his truest friend.

If I'd only been a tomato you see,
I would have at least felt the embrace of my father in some
way to me.

There's a great caveat, though, because we as human beings
can always come ashore and have new beginnings. The
human spirit is amazingly tenacious with strength and hope,
but it is not something someone else can do for us. We

have the distinct privilege of finding our own way through our journey.

It is my hope that readers of this book will not only be encouraged but provoked to wholeness. What's unique is how my definition of wholeness might be different than yours. Even though each of us are distinctly unique in so many ways, we are also the same in how we need to both give and receive genuine love. Hope needs to be the train we ride every day with purpose being the destination.

The Fruit of Wholeness

We need genuine love,
Peace in the midst of our circumstances,
Joy that leads us into the future,
Patience that establishes the way,
Goodness that flavors the journey,
Kindness that makes the path smooth,
Faithfulness that heralds the integrity of who we are,
Gentleness that makes friends
And self-control that doesn't make enemies

Scene 25: Trauma

Over the years I have come to realize and appreciate how the most valuable tool in relationship to others is being present. This is even more important when building rapport and trust with someone to assist them on their journey of healing from trauma. It means deep, active listening without judgment and without interruption (something I still struggle with in many of my relationships).

When we're just willing to be present for people, to take in who they are in that moment and their situation, without judgment, then we release those people to be genuine and find themselves in the midst of their situation. I have seen time after time how this dynamic plays out into positive outcomes, particularly in trauma intervention situations.

It occurs to me this is why we have two ears but only one mouth—because we need to be people who can really hear and listen with both intent and purpose. Being fully present with someone makes that moment of time with them a sacred space. There are very specific ingredients that go into the recipe for being present in a magical, healing kind of way. Three stories will illustrate the point.

It was about 1:30 AM when I received a dispatch call, was given an address, and was told it was a suicide. As I approached the location there were dozens of sheriff cars lining the streets. The home where the incident took place was taped off as detectives were at work.

I found the Duty Sergeant and introduced myself and showed him my badge. He told me the person I was to connect with was the wife of the man who committed suicide. He said, "Before you meet her though, I want you to be aware of the nature of what took place. There was an argument, the husband grabbed his 45-caliber pistol, stuck it in his mouth, and blew the back of his head off within two feet of his wife, causing his body to tumble down the stairs."

He directed me down the street where there were three officers currently with her and gave me her first name. When

I got there she was yelling and screaming rather colorful superlatives. Two female and one male officer were trying to keep her safe. Initially I just stood and watched. As they moved up and down the block, I would move with them.

She eventually ran out of steam and made eye contact with me. The officers who were with her explained to her who I was and why I was there. She looked at me with a fierce look and said, "What the hell do you want? And what are you going to tell me?" I introduced myself and said I was just there to be with her. And with that she took off rambling again down the block. I pulled aside one of the female officers and asked if there was anyone else in the house. They didn't even know yet. It turns out there was a newborn infant asleep in their room and I could hear dogs barking. Her three dogs were in the backyard.

When the woman finished another round of ranting and made eye contact with me again, I asked her if she could sit on the grass with me. I said to her, "Who do you know who you trust that can help you right now?" She gave me the name of a person I later found out was her boss at work. Digging through her purse she found her phone. I asked her if I could use it to get the phone number of her boss. I said to her, "We need to call your friend. Are you ready?" She exclaimed, "I have no idea what to say." I said, "It doesn't matter. Just call her and I'll help."

We spoke with the boss, who said she'd get her HR person and both of them would come immediately to help however they could. The police confirmed there was a baby asleep in the house and that was something that needed to be figured out. I explained to them that her boss and her HR person were *en route* and they were coming to help.

In a little while, two women showed up and introduced themselves as her boss and the HR person. They immediately asked what they could do. I said, "It's very important she get away from the crime scene, as just being around it makes her want to burn the house down." Within a few minutes we put a plan in place, but there was another situation to figure out—the dogs.

I went to my vehicle and grabbed the extra dog leashes I always have with me. The baby was now in the car, with formula and necessary items for the next few days. I asked the officer to get the dogs and I would stay here. Her boss said the dogs could come to her house, but she couldn't transport them and the baby in her vehicle. She called a male coworker who could come pick up the dogs and take them to her home.

When the officers came out with three large dogs, the woman immediately broke away from us to be with her dogs. She broke down in tears as she kissed and hugged her dogs and they licked her with great affection. She was a different person the *instant* she *reconnected* with her dogs, who were absolutely fully present for her in her trauma. I ended up putting the dogs in the back of my car to wait for their transportation to arrive.

She asked me, "Can I come over and sit in your car with them?" The back of my vehicle is a large dog bed made up for my dog. They were beside themselves, smelling every inch of it. She came to my car, I let her in the passenger side. I gave her the personal space she needed. I could tell by the gesturing that she was deeply expressing herself as she talked with the dogs. It was time for her to leave with her baby and the transportation for the dogs arrived. She got out of the vehicle and came over and gave me a big hug. With a calmness in her eyes in the midst of a terrible evening, she said, "Thank you."

The nature of this kind of emergency trauma response doesn't involve any follow-up, it's just getting a person through the initial immediate aftermath when all is utter confusion. I don't know what happened to her in the following days, but I did get a phone call from dispatch asking if the woman's boss could call me. A couple days later, I had a very heartfelt telephone conversation with her in which she said things were moving forward even though nothing would be normal for the woman for a long time. Yes, *there is power in being present.*

These trauma intervention calls almost always deal with a death, and it's rarely a natural death. More common are suicides, shootings, drug overdoses, automobile accidents, and so on.

****

On another early morning I received a phone call from a neighboring community Sheriff. I was given the name, address, and the nature of the call—an abduction. When I arrived, I pulled over amidst at least thirty police cars, some marked and some unmarked. I found out later it was the FBI. I connected with the lieutenant in charge and he told me the man of the household had been abducted and my client would be the wife. He escorted me in and shadowing us was a young man who was a trainee of the Sheriff's department. Entering the house, I could see the wife was very upset and talking with someone on the phone. Across the room I could see their dining room table was full of grocery bags they were going to take on their trip the next day to Mexico to visit their newly constructed vacation home.

The person she was talking with on the phone was in fact her husband. The lieutenant asked her to put it on speaker phone. What we were about to hear was so unbelievable I thought it had to be a syndicated crime drama, since it couldn't be real. After a bit I explained to her who I was and why I was there. I asked if it would be alright for me to talk with her husband. The only information we had at the time was that he had been abducted.

He had left early that morning to pick up some additional items they needed for their trip the next day. He received a phone call from people who claimed to have his sixteen-year-old daughter, who they named, and a girl's voice in the background began to say, "Daddy, daddy, help me!"

He was instructed to go to his bank and withdraw $50,000 or they would rape his daughter and slit her throat. He was told he was being watched and tracked electronically, including every phone call he made. If he didn't do exactly as they said, his daughter would be dead.

He was instructed to wire money to specific locations, each of them having a different routing number. He was told he was to destroy the receipts after he had taken a picture of them to forward to a different phone number (all single-use burner phones). This nightmare went on for eleven hours, forcing him to travel over 200 miles as he was given different instructions and information each time, all with the purpose of terrifying him. They also made reference to his wife and son by name and said they had an accomplice watching them at their house.

It was then late at night and they instructed him to go to a drive-up coastal motel two hours north of his house. Each phone call deliberately provided specific information about him and his immediate family to make sure there was no doubt in his mind that everything happening was true. They told him what hotel and which room to go to and to not talk with anyone. There would be a key above the door.

He realized by this time his phone was about to die and needed to be charged. He explained he wanted to go down to his truck to get his phone charger so he could charge it overnight. As he went to his truck he found his iPad, and even though he thought he was being observed, he quickly leaned over the seat and slipped it underneath his coat and returned to his room. His kidnappers said they would call him in the morning. Using his iPad and a newly opened social network account, he posted, "I've been abducted, here's where I'm at, I'm in X room. I need help!"

The police said they received several phone calls immediately. Three squad cars showed up, broke down the hotel door, shoved the man face down on his bed, and hand-cuffed him behind. They had no idea who he was.

By the time I ended up talking with him, he had already been with the police for an hour. Only after lengthy discussions with me, the authorities, and the FBI, did it all finally make sense. The police assured him his daughter was at home and his whole family was safe. I asked him what he wanted to do and he just kept saying, "I gotta get home! I gotta get home!" After the EMTs arrived to check him out and he got something to eat, he was given the all-clear to return home.

The next two hours was a live conversation that I had with him, stoplight by stoplight, on the freeway, off the freeway, street by street, as he made his way home. I wanted to make sure he was safe to drive. He kept saying to me, "Just keep talking to me."

It was now about four hours after I initially arrived. He finally drove up to the house, all of the police vehicles were gone except the lieutenant and his trainee. The man was in emotional turmoil, and rather loudly expressing himself, terrified that his nightmare wasn't really over. I accompanied him upstairs so he could look in on his daughter, safe and soundly sleeping. He was again overcome with emotion and had to go back downstairs. This whole time, his two dogs were scratching and whining to come out and greet their master who was finally back home. At last the dogs were allowed in. They were a gift to him from his wife several anniversaries ago, a pair of siblings (brother and sister). These two dogs engulfed the man with kisses and whining.

He wrapped his arms around his beloved dogs and just cried and cried.

His whole persona had changed from that of *terror* to that of being *comforted*. And somehow in the midst of a night that never could have happened but did, things were going to be okay. He began to laugh and turned to his wife and said, "Well, I don't think we are going to Mexico tomorrow."

When the Lieutenant decided it was finally time for him to leave, the trainee pulled me aside, having observed the whole night, and said, "I thought I wanted to be a Sheriff, but boy, I want to do what you do." Later it was discovered that the reason his abductors had so much information about his family was because they had filled out detailed applications for the construction of their vacation home in Mexico—a source of information at the center of an identify-theft syndicate.

People don't need to be told what to do or how to do it, they don't need information. They need to be connected with, as a relief valve for who they are in that moment. Yes, being present is an art form and so needed in our society today, especially with the social dynamics currently expressing themselves in our world. I'll tell one more story to finish making this point.

****

It was an early morning off the shores of the Australian coast, a favorite place where surfers convened to relax before their workday was to start. There was a middle-aged man paddling about, beyond the usual breakers, awaiting the time his usual mammoth ride would appear. He saw a dark figure moving in the water towards him. He decided to stop making movement and be still. A very large shark appeared and circled him several times, so close it caused a rippling and movement in the water that rocked the surfboard back and forth. And then, nothing. The shark had disappeared from his view. With a sigh of relief his terror diminished and he began to slowly paddle towards shore.

Then, in an instant, there was a rushing of the water behind, similar to the movement just as you reach the crest of a wave. The movement increased with an immense force as he plunged forward, stronger than he had ever experienced even on his best ride. He knew the shark had come back for him.

But he felt nothing. Were his nerves severed so that he couldn't feel anything? He was sure he'd been ripped apart. After all, he once saw his best friend's girlfriend attacked by a shark while paddling. The shark bit off her entire her right arm. Weeks later he talked with her and she said except for the bleeding and the fact that her arm was gone, she literally hadn't felt a thing.

Within an instant he was pushed right in front of the crest of a wave, which hurled him to shore. There was much commotion as several other surfers began to approach him as they realized what had taken place. His best friend, the one whose girlfriend had lost her arm, approached him first and said that the EMTs were on their way.

He didn't want to look, so he said to his best friend, "How bad is it?" With a smile on his face he said, "You're going to need a new surfboard." You see, the shark had consumed the end of the longboard that he was on. It was his father's original longboard, and this was in the days when surfboards seemed oversized compared to those today.

When Lifeguard Rescue arrived they saw how the whole end of the surfboard was gone. The bite was so large and the teeth spaced in such a way that it was clear it was an adult Great White Shark. After figuring out how he was laying and the length of his body in relationship to the surfboard, it was obvious that the shark missed his feet by mere inches. He had no injuries, at least not physically.

A couple hours later he found himself sitting on the edge of the water as it lapped against the shore, with his surfboard across his lap, thinking about his father. He began to reminisce over the good and bad times. The next day he went to his father's graveside and had a long conversation he'd never had with his dad when he was alive. The interaction from the event so dramatically impacted his life that it caused him to live differently from that day forward. It would be wonderful if all interactions with animals were as loving and comforting as a dog. Unfortunately, predators think otherwise.

Scene 26: Anchors Away...

Living in San Diego for many years affords the opportunity for many different outings. The Maritime Museum at the harbor is by far one of the most unique attractions for those who visit our city. Of all the different things to be seen from submarines to triple-mast historic sailing ships, the clear standout is the WWII Midway Aircraft Carrier.

It has a flight deck larger than three football fields weighing 100,000 tons. Rising to the height of six stories, its docked presence expresses a formidable witness of history and vision.

What I find especially fascinating are the two massive anchors found on either side of the bow of the ship. The anchors weigh twenty tons each (that's 40,000 pounds each). Anchors like that still have to be attached to a chain. In this case, each individual link of the chain weighs 156 pounds, and there is nearly 2,000 feet of that chain on board.

Looking up from the dock the anchors protrude from either side of the bow, like the eyes of a dragon lizard from the Galapagos Islands. When the anchors are deployed they provide safety and stability to this huge city on the water.

This makes me ponder about us, the human inhabitants of this world. What do we look to in order to keep us safe and secure?

For me it is the *hope* that I cherish and keep before me every day. It is also interesting to me how *hope* can be both a noun and a verb. Hope as a verb means to anticipate, await, expect, watch for or envision. It's about wanting something to be the case or wanting something to happen. Hope as a noun means a belief or feeling of expectation or desire for a particular outcome.

For me to put my hope in something, it's got to be trustworthy and constant. We can be people who trust in our jobs, bank accounts, career—the things that we can accomplish and produce and make better. While those are realistic things in which we can place trust and hope, they are not constant. They are ever-changing and fluid. So it seems logical to me that if I place my hope in something that can change, I am essentially negating the very meaning of hope as I understand it.

Looking back at the Midway, the reason the anchors provide safety and security is because what they are tethered to is *unmovable*. The question this poses for me is this: How can I place my hope, my anticipation, the things I watch for, in something that's not constant? For instance, we don't say, "I hope the sun comes up tomorrow!" Because it does every day. There's no reason to think it won't.

What is there in my life that *is* constant, that I can depend on, that I can anticipate and expect will be there all the time, like clockwork? Or maybe there simply isn't anything with that kind of constancy that dramatically affects my life. But when we look around our universe, the plant kingdom, how photosynthesis works, how osmosis works, the very nature of physics, we see how we depend on so many things being constant in order to just survive. A system to take in carbon dioxide and put out oxygen just so we can breathe. So it seems like there is a counterbalance that *is* constant and predictable, like clockwork, and this something forms the bedrock foundation of our very existence—what we eat, how we breathe, how we literally survive. To illustrate this point, here's a true story:

Daniel was an up and coming lawyer who graduated *magnum cum laude* in his class. He came from a very wealthy family. His father was a neurologist and his mother was running for office, facing off against the incumbent governor of the state in the upcoming election. Daniel was living on the east coast, working for a very large, prestigious law firm with an impeccable record, including winning 94% of its cases. One day, he got a phone call from his aunt (his mother's sister) that there had been a car accident that left his father dead and his mother on a ventilator.

The next year was understandably very difficult for him as he tried to make sense of what was going on. His firm was considering making him a partner, but one of his colleagues went out of his way to block his promotion. The ensuing dynamics set in place were designed to not only steal his promotion but get him fired—and it worked. He lost his job, his car, and all the furnishings in his Manhattan flat. His world literally fell apart.

I met him twenty years after all that happened. He was unkempt, obese, and reeked of body odor from lack of attention to hygiene. His *was* had become his *is* and he was deeply stuck. I followed his whereabouts for a couple years and then it seemed like he just disappeared.

Yes, our lives can change in an instant. We see it in the news every day. The things in which we've placed our hope for the future, whether it's a career or some other pathway to success, are dashed to pieces in the blink of an eye. And so I ask you: What do you find hope in? What is the constant you know you can count on in your life?

Seeking answers to these questions with genuine sincerity can lead you on a path of discovery that will utterly and profoundly change your life, birthing a new reality for you every bit as magical as Henrietta the caterpillar transforming into a beautiful iridescent blue butterfly.

Scene 27: Bringing it Home

It wasn't until Jimmy's series of hospitalizations that he discovered he was dyslexic and had been his whole life. This had a lot to do with why he didn't like to read. In fact, in a high school drama class, he was supposed to read Shylock's speech in *The Merchant of Venice* by William Shakespeare. But because reading was so difficult, he opted instead to memorize it, and always remembered it throughout his entire life.

Shylock, a Jewish merchant, was incensed with the Christians of his day. His response throughout the speech represents his relationship to the Christian community. He is talking about the similarities both cultures represent:

To bait fish withal: if it will feed nothing else,
it will feed my revenge. He hath disgraced me, and
hindered me half a million; laughed at my losses,
mocked at my gains, scorned my nation, thwarted my
bargains, cooled my friends, heated mine
enemies; and what's his reason? I am a Jew. Hath
not a Jew eyes? hath not a Jew hands, organs,
dimensions, senses, affections, passions? fed with
the same food, hurt with the same weapons, subject

to the same diseases, healed by the same means,
warmed and cooled by the same winter and summer, as
a Christian is? If you prick us, do we not bleed?
if you tickle us, do we not laugh? if you poison
us, do we not die? and if you wrong us, shall we not
revenge? If we are like you in the rest, we will
resemble you in that. If a Jew wrong a Christian,
what is his humility? Revenge. If a Christian
wrong a Jew, what should his sufferance be by
Christian example? Why, revenge. The villainy you
teach me, I will execute, and it shall go hard but I
will better the instruction.

It highlights in such an important way how we all have just
as much if not more in common than the differences we all
too often focus on, whether it's politics, our upbringing, our
social organizations, our culture and its beliefs, all of which
have led to who we are in the present moment. We have an
inalienable right to freely be who we are regardless of what
the world thinks about us.

Have you ever wondered how you came to be who you are?
Was it your childhood experiences, the beliefs of your parents, your associations as you grew up, the education you
received, the profession you chose to follow? It is indeed all
of the above, plus many other things that have contributed
to make up who you are right now as you read this.

You are a unique individual comprised of what you think,
the way you act, your cultural heritage, your experiences,
what you like, and what you dislike. Do you know what you
believe and why you believe it? Have you ever been given

the opportunity to have conversation with a total stranger in which you had the freedom to truly be who you are and have the other person be fully present and listen without judgment and without interruption or the need to express their perspective? It's an opportunity that rarely presents itself these days, and yet is needed more than ever for that very reason.

We all have the need to give love and receive it. We understand pain (both physical and emotional), anger, and disappointment. The echoes of anxiety and fear can resound long after the incidents that initiated them. Many have had to face the *Dragon of Depression*. We understand feelings of inadequacy as well as victory. We have wandered down pathways of feeling lost and alone as well as climbing to the heights of purpose and accomplishment.

The absolute need for peace overshadows our lives with the grace of an eraser that allows us to start over, which is forgiveness, and it benefits most the person *giving* it than the person receiving it.

Can you agree we are all very much alike despite our individual uniqueness?

Looking back at Jimmy and his butterfly companion, it was Henrietta's presence in Jimmy's life that had the profound effect of enabling him to not only survive but thrive in spite all the challenges he experienced in his life. Everyone not only deserves but deeply *needs* to have a Henrietta in their life. The good news is that you can. All you have to do is *choose* what you're going to believe.

After many years of talking with thousands of people, I realize I have never met a person who does not have a stand, belief, or posture of some kind regarding what they believe about God.

Jimmy's father believed there wasn't one. Jimmy only discovered years after his father's passing how it was the incident of his grandfather committing suicide in the basement of the Lutheran Church that both sparked and cemented his dad's posture towards God. Through subsequent conversations with his mother and reading letters from long ago, Jimmy also discovered what was once upon a time his dad's dedication to and love for God.

Now I ask for your willingness to *listen* without judgement and without interruption, to be fully present as we go back to when Jimmy was ten years old in the abandoned golf course and napping at the creek.

****

There was a majestic oak tree in the middle of a valley where a developer was going to create a "one of a kind golf course experience." In the process of acquiring the needed permits, he discovered that the historical society had placed restrictions on the removal or relocation of this tree. As far back as they had records it seemed the tree had always been there. The developer would have to make major adjustments to his plans in order to accommodate the tree.

The girth of the oak tree, with its meandering branches, cast a shadow which covered an immense landmass. Standing at the base looking skyward captures the majesty of its strong and intricate structure. Its stout branches and limbs extended from the trunk, reaching out to the world around it. And yet amidst the strong elements of its structure were all the tiny, fragile twigs from which leaves grow. Without its foliage, it would be little more than a skeleton. Despite its gnarly appearance, it announced its purposeful, majestic presence.

And on one particular twig among thousands there hung this small sack, the cocoon in which a caterpillar had instinctively encased itself in order to enter its metamorphosis, its rebirth as an entirely new creature—a beautiful butterfly.

****

The tree, of course, is God—always there, always reaching out to us, inviting us to be in relationship with our Creator and to be embraced by the branches of divine love, grace, and mercy, to shine light into the darkest corners of the world and our lives.

The caterpillar in the cocoon is *you*. We each spin our own webs of entrapment, but the cocoon is not permanent. You can emerge from it. Just like every caterpillar who goes through its metamorphosis, God has provided the mechanism by which you can peel away your cocoon and be born anew, and that mechanism is Jesus Christ, the ultimate revelation of God and savior of the world. In Jimmy's story, the butterfly represents the Holy Spirit, the divine presence that brings peace and comfort throughout life's journey. It is this divine trinity of Creator, Christ, and Comforter in which we can place our trust and hope, for nothing else can ever be as constant as the triune God of the universe.

****

Thank you for listening, even if what you've just read doesn't fit with how you currently see yourself. But I also hope with all my heart that you will make the choice that will put you on the pathway of a journey—a deeply personal relationship with God who will embrace you as you are. It's not about going to church, it's about opening your heart to your Creator, Christ, and Comforter, allowing yourself to be transformed into a new creation, with a different reality as a person who is fully present in this world and living in love, joy, peace, patience, kindness, goodness, faithfulness, gentleness, and self-control.

Romans 14:17 (NIV) sums it up nicely: "For the kingdom of God is not a matter of eating and drinking, but of righteousness, peace and joy in the Holy Spirit."

Will you allow yourself the freedom to respond instinctively to this God who is patiently waiting for you with open arms?

Oh! By the way, the mariner's compass is... the Word of God!

And the secret fort is... the innermost desires of your heart; the lamppost of your past that shines into your future.

ENJOY & BUCKEL UP!

EPILOGUE

As James made his way to the theatre to see the next performance of *Cocoons in the Midst: An Unfolding Journey, a Choice*, he faintly heard a woman's voice behind him calling, "James? James?" Then more emphatically, "Jimmy! Jimmy it's me!" It was being called Jimmy that jostled him to attention. He used to be called Jimmy many years ago but felt as if he'd been going by James nearly as long.

He couldn't immediately place the woman before him, but it was clearly someone who knew him a long time ago. He was intrigued. "Shall we attend this performance together?" he asked her. She nodded her head with a warm smile and took his arm. At that very moment James felt a familiar fluttering at the back of his neck.

The woman at his side exclaimed, "Why, look! Jimmy, there's the most beautiful iridescent blue butterfly on your shoulder. I've never seen anything like it."

James glanced at his life-long companion and smiled his hello to her before she fluttered off as they entered the theatre. "That's my friend, Henrietta. It's a long story. I'll tell you all about her after the show."

They took their seats in the auditorium, which was filled to capacity and buzzing with excited conversation. When the lights blinked twice to indicate the show was about to start, an immediate and profound hush fell over the audience. As the house lights slowly dimmed, James realized he didn't have a program. He glanced around and noticed no one else had one either. *How very odd*, he thought.

Before he could reflect further on what must have been an intentional decision on the part of the production team, the curtain rose and the lights came up on a stage that was bare except for a young boy, perhaps ten years old at most, who was holding an old canning jar containing a bright green caterpillar. A wave of recognition and memories washed over James unlike anything he had ever before experienced.

ABOUT THE AUTHOR

KEN LIVES IN SAN DIEGO, California with his wife Andrea and their therapy dog, Ranger. Ken is a Holistic Health Practitioner and Andrea is a Homeopath extraordinaire. They founded The Wellness Advantage more than twenty years ago as an alternative healthcare practice with international influence.

The past sixty years have provided Ken with unique experiences to assist people of all ages through diverse settings such as group homes for disadvantaged youth, federal SOHC programs (specialized out of home care) for target offender youths, bereavement facilitation, and trauma intervention with first responders. At this point in time, he works one-on-one with people experiencing schizophrenia, TBI (traumatic brain injury) dementia, Alzheimer's, strokes, Parkinson's, and end-of-life dynamics, all the while with a pastor's heart.

In this phase of life, Ken finds himself sharing his passion for wholeness with anyone who will listen. He moves in a variety of local settings (support groups, conventions, churches) and also travels nationally and globally to share his experiences of facilitating healing and wholeness. He was most recently scheduled to speak about *The Other Side of Trauma... Birthing* and what he calls "Cocooning" at the 7th Annual Congress on Trauma in Florence, Italy in July 2020—an event that had to be rescheduled because of the novel coronavirus and COVID-19 global pandemic.

Ken's passion is sharing a message of hope for people everywhere to discover and embrace the resources within them through the journey of being human. He and Ranger are a certified therapy team, working together to bring comfort and healing to people in need.

To contact Ken:
1-760-535-5893
Ken@wellnessinliving.com